Praise for S

"In *Sy's Gift* Patricia Owens takes us to a small town in coastal South Carolina, where residents are battening down the hatches in preparation for a hurricane, where everyone knows everyone else and gossip is as certain as sunrise. Cameron Patterson, widow and mother of an obstreperous 20-year-old adopted daughter, is shocked by the sudden appearance of her late husband's illegitimate son, Michael Duncan. Cameron's daughter Nell resents Michael from the outset and is suspicious of his motives. But Cameron finds in Michael a connection with her dead husband Sy that is both mystifying and comforting. Owens, who is particularly adept at creating a sense of place, gives us an unforgettable cast of characters and an intriguing plot in a setting so real one can smell the salt air and feel the inescapable heat. With intertwining stories of love, heartbreak, and determination, *Sy's Gift* is a rollicking good ride and a fine read."

    ___Anna Jean Mayhew author of
    The Dry Grass of August

The 2011 Sir Walter Raleigh Award for Fiction

"Sy's Gift is a gift to readers who love intriguing plot twists and fascinating, quirky characters. Ms. Owens has mastered the authentic southern narrative style and written a gem of a book."

    ___Helen E. Johnson, author
Don't Tell Me What To Do, Just Send Money:
The Essential Parenting Guide to the College Years

All rights reserved by Patricia C. Owens, 902 E. Franklin St., Chapel Hill, N.C. 27514 - powens5@nc.rr.com

This is a work of fiction. Although the insights are based on experience, all names, places and persons are products of the author's imagination.

ISBN-978-1470072476
1. Lowcountry South Carolina 2.1986 3. Fiction
4, Melungeon History 5. Art

Sy's Gift

A Novel by

Patricia Cavanaugh Owens

Mercury Books of Chapel Hill, North Carolina

ACKNOWLEDGEMENTS

Special thanks to North Carolina based artist David G. Snyder for the use of his beautiful painting *NC Intercoastal #1* as a cover image. It captures the feel of the region and the novel. Also, thanks to Joe Rowand and the Joe Rowand Art Gallery, Chapel Hill, N. C. that represents David and secured the use of the painting for the book.

Heartfelt thanks to Merri Edwards, Helen Johnson and Dorothy Hodges.

And to Anna Jean Mayhew for her years of patient coaching.

Thursday

September 12, 1989

Cameron locked the gallery door and walked across the hot gravel parking lot to her car. Overhead, a stagnant sky gave no hint of the hurricane churning in the Atlantic. But she could feel it, and she could smell its rancid breath. Unless the storm changed course it would hit somewhere along the U.S. coast a week to ten days from now. The 5000 residents of Hobetown, South Carolina, had been warned to prepare. There'd been a time when these warnings were ignored. Not anymore. In the last five years four major hurricanes had hit the East Coast. Experts blamed global warming for these natural disasters, but the old men who sat on the cast-off church pew in front of the drugstore disagreed. The earth got hot, and the earth got cold—and one time it even flooded. That's just the way it was and ever would be.

The whine of Ernestine Gentry's window fan drifted across the street as it strained to remove the dank air trapped inside her house. Cameron pictured the old woman rocking on the porch, waiting for the breeze that blew off the water each day about this time.

Cameron set the air on high in the seven-year-old BMW convertible that Sy had bought two months before his death. She should have gotten rid of it a long time ago—too expensive to keep running. But this was one of the few tangible reminders left of Sy, and she couldn't bring herself to let it go.

Houses she passed on the ten-block drive to her home, mostly two-story, eighteenth-century colonials, like the one she lived in, had shutters closed or heavy drapes drawn across the windows to block the afternoon sun. No amount of air conditioning could keep these relics free from mildew. Decades of humidity permeated the thick boards of local heart pine, hand-sawn and constructed by slave labor. Northerners complained about the mustiness, but natives had grown up with it. The scent of the South, they called it.

Cameron pulled into her driveway and sat a moment, looking over the expanse of emerald lawn kept lush by the thunderstorms that rolled through each afternoon. Mounds of red petunias and blue salvia framed the porch, and scarlet cannas as tall as her head wandered down the side of the house toward the kitchen.

Nell's car was gone. Good. She'd been im-impossible to live with these last couple of months.

Cameron picked up a note by the phone: "You've got a message on save."

"Damn it," she said to the empty room, annoyed that Nell continued to listen to her messages, when it was Nell who'd insisted that each have their own phone. Nell, who didn't want her mother answering her calls.

Cameron tossed the note on the table. No point getting upset over a phone message. She had nothing to hide.

The voice beneath the save button sounded young and vaguely familiar.

"Hello, this is Michael Duncan in Hartford Connecticut. I'm going to be in South Carolina, tomorrow and would like to stop by and talk to you about the Patterson family. Please call me back." He left his number.

Why would he call her? Sy's family wasn't from around here.

Later that evening, when it cooled down, Cameron took the phone to the porch, curious to find out what Michael Duncan wanted. The same pleasant voice answered.

"Thanks for returning my call. I'll be down your way tomorrow. Would it be convenient for me to stop by?"

"I'm not sure I can help you, but I'll be in my gallery on Sunrise Avenue most of the day."

"Thanks so much. I'll see you tomorrow afternoon." He hung up before she could ask why he chose Hobetown to do research. If you wanted to know about the Pattersons, you'd go to North

Carolina.

Cameron was turning out the lights when she heard the back door slam. Nell walked into the living room holding a cup of yogurt, and sank into a chair, drawing her tiny body into a ball. Her hair, pink in front and ink black in back, was cropped short except for a stringy rat tail that hung down one shoulder. Loops and studs rimmed her ears. She had on those ridiculous army boots. A butterfly tattoo across the back of her thin neck, with each wing spreading almost to her chin, stopped Cameron. She hated tattoos and Nell knew it.

"It's not permanent," Nell giggled, "Yet. Just wanted to see what it would look like."

Cameron looked at her daughter, trying to understand. "What about your hair?"

"Don't be such a crab. It washes out."

"If you spent half as much time trying to look good as you do looking different, you'd be so pretty."

"I'll never be tall and blonde and beautiful like you," Nell snapped. "I'm short, flat-chested and ugly. Look at my stringy hair." She tugged at her scalp.

"I'm going to bed. Turn out the lights."

Nell whirled around. "Why do you say that every night? I always turn out the lights, don't I?" She lifted a spoon of yogurt to her glossy black lips. "Who's that guy on the phone?"

"Someone interested in Patterson history.

Wants to come by the gallery tomorrow."

"Probably more crap like that stuff the other day."

"What stuff?"

"Something in the mail about the Pattersons having strange diseases. I opened it by mistake. Sorry." Nell started to get up, but Cameron leaned over, blocking her way.

"Why didn't you show it to me?"

"Because there aren't any Pattersons left around here except us."

Cameron didn't move.

"Just junk mail. I put it in the recycle bin. What's the big deal?"

"Get it."

Nell stomped out of the room and returned with a crumpled wad. She thrust it at Cameron. "Satisfied?"

Cameron smoothed out the pages. An organization called Melungeon Cousins had written inquiring if Sylvester Patterson or members of his family had developed symptoms similar to those described in the enclosed brochure, the result of three different genetic diseases.

"That's one of those shows that tries to find people's parents, isn't it?" Nell said.

"No. Descendants of people called Melungeons. Appalachian settlers. They wanted to know if your dad's family had certain diseases."

"Why are they writing us?"

"Patterson is a Melungeon name," Cameron

replied. "They're collecting information."

Nell wrinkled her nose. "Sounds fishy to me. The guy on the phone, is he one of them?"

"I don't know."

"Bet he's looking for adopted people's real mothers. When they're reunited with their birth mother, they get all kinds of prizes—a car, money. Maybe I should do that."

Cameron sat on the arm of the sofa and looked down at her daughter. "Are you serious? That's the second time you've mentioned your birth mother recently."

"Why shouldn't I find her? Do you know where she is?"

"No. I could make some inquiries if you want me to."

Nell shrugged. "Why not?"

Cameron walked to her bedroom, shaken and wondering if Nell really wanted to find her birth mother or was this just another way of getting attention. She loved her daughter, but she didn't always like her, especially these last months. Nell was the cause of Cameron's breakup with Mark, the engineer who'd come to build Hobetown's new bridge and the only man she'd been interested in since Sy's death. She found it hard to look at her daughter and not be angry.

Friday, September 13

MICHAEL DUNCAN

Michael had hoped he was finally free of the fever and pain he'd suffered from childhood. Then three months ago he developed skin lesions, angry red blisters over much of his body. Such pain in his chest that every breath he drew felt like a knife stabbing him. He'd made excuses to be out of his law office when he was the sickest, working nights and weekends to make up the time.

When the symptoms persisted he made an appointment with a rheumatologist.

"Looks like FMF, Familial Mediterranean Fever, a rare genetic disease," the doctor had said, when the test results came back. "Are your parents living?"

"My mother. Never knew my father."

"Is there a family history of this disease? Or Mediterranean ancestry?"

"None at all," Michael replied. "We're Irish. I couldn't have the gene."

The doctor smiled. "Anyone can have it.

Millions of people carry it unknowingly."

Michael was doubtful, but intrigued; Mediterranean?

The doctor continued. "FMF is regressive; both parents have to pass the gene to their offspring. The same as Cystic Fibrosis and Sickle Cell Anemia. I'd like to start you on Colchicine. It may not stop the disease, but it will help slow down a serious complication called Systemic Amyloidosis. There are side effects like pain in the back and genitals, swelling, weakness, vomiting, diarrhea, yellowing of the skin. That's just some of them, or, if you're lucky, none of them."

"What happens if I don't take it?"

"If you don't have FMF, nothing. I have to be honest with you, your heart shows damage and Amyloidosis could be fatal."

"Jesus, you don't leave me much choice."

"If you think you can locate your father, or his family history, we can wait, but not too long."

As soon as Michael got home from the doctor's office, he called his grandfather, Big Mike, in Boston where he and Michael's mother had lived together since Michael was born. He loved them both, but as hard as he tried he couldn't understand his mother. All her moves were calculated according to astrology, karma, past life regressions and psychic readers. He'd stopped asking about his father years ago. It upset her so he lost interest. He had his grandfather, a wiry little man, born in the coalfields of West Virginia, and that was enough.

"What do you know about my father?" Michael asked Big Mike.

"Not much, son. I never met him. Your ma never said much about him except his name was Patterson and he was from down South somewhere."

Having unloaded the news from the doctor, he continued. "I need to locate my father or some of his family to get their history. Mother's got to help me."

"Before I'd worry about all that, I'd think about starting the medication."

"With side effects like impotence?"

Big Mike took a deep breath. "You got a right to be upset. Let me see what I can find out."

The following weekend, Michael drove from Hartford to Boston. Big Mike sat rocking on the porch, waiting. "Sit down a minute," he said. "Learned some things you ought to know. Looked up FMF at the library and found out that folks from a county in Tennessee have a whole lot of it. They're descendants of people called Melungeons, first white folks to settle the Appalachian Mountains. Couple years back a bunch of them, ones that was sick and the doctors didn't know why, got together and started an organization to try to figure it out. Found out they had diseases that Mediterranean people get. Didn't none of them think they had Mediterranean blood." He paused and shook his head. "That's where my mother come from, where the Melungeons settled, Newman's Ridge, Tennessee."

"I inherited it from you?"

"Afraid you did." Big Mike stopped rocking. "My mother was a pretty woman, dark skin, eyes black as coal. First time my daddy saw her he called her Gypsy. Your ma takes after her a whole lot, in looks, anyway."

"It takes both parents to pass it on. If my father wasn't a carrier, I couldn't have the disease. Did you tell Mother?"

Big Mike nodded. "She didn't act surprised, but I saw her reading that book I brought home from the library. Think she contacted someone about the Melungeons. She's inside waiting for you."

Michael walked into the house prepared to hear a lecture about how this had all been foretold—the usual bullshit he'd grown up hearing. She sat quietly, draped in a shawl, glassy-eyed, staring out the window with all expression drained from her face. Her long black hair, streaked with white, hung loosely around her face, the way she always looked when she'd taken too much "nerve medicine."

"Big Mike told me the diagnosis. I'm sorry, son. Why do you question it?" she asked.

"Because I'm not Middle Eastern."

"Of course you are. Remember? Your past life. The shaman told you."

"You expect me to start a radical treatment

based on what a half-crazy, juiced-up jungle man said when I was fifteen?"

She closed her eyes and dropped her head, a gesture he's seen so often when her feelings were hurt. "Your father and I were together in a past life, but our destiny wasn't fulfilled until we met again and had you, our son. You saw it all in the regression. I know you remember."

"That was a dream induced by hypnosis and suggestion."

"Accept your karma, Michael. Begin the treatment."

Michael stood up and walked to the door, then came back. "Was my father a Southerner?"

The question startled her. "Why do you ask?"

"Didn't Big Mike talk to you about the Melungeons? His mother? Maybe my father was a descendant too."

She looked up, but he wasn't even sure she saw him. "I must concentrate," she murmured, and pressed her palms together. "Time, I need a little time."

The next day he drove back to Connecticut, frustrated because his mother had gone into one of her meditative states and barely spoke to him or Big Mike the rest of the day.

Four days later he received her letter.
Dear Michael,
It is clear to me now. I should have told you

about your father. This unexpected illness you have has changed everything. Forgive me.

In 1964 I was attending secretarial school in Boston and working at the Metaphysical Center. Your father was in school at BU. We were together for a year. I thought it would be forever. It didn't work out that way. At first I was hurt, but later I realized this is how it was supposed to be. He and I met so you could be born. His name was William Sylvester Patterson and he was from Hobetown, South Carolina. He died seven years ago in a boating accident. Not long after he left Boston he got married. I never saw him again nor did I tell him about you. He was an honorable man and would have felt obligated, and I didn't want him or his family interfering in our lives. When you were born I called you Sy's Gift although I named you Michael, after Big Mike. I'm sorry for the pain this causes you, but I'd never be sorry for bringing you into the world. You're the best thing that ever happened to me. I hope you understand.

Your devoted mother

Enclosed is a picture of your father (the tall, handsome one) me, and a friend of his from Hobetown.

Michael had put the letter in his desk drawer, and every day since he'd taken it out and looked at the picture. What kind of a man had Sy Patterson been? Honorable, his mother called him. The only way to find out was to go down there and talk to the people who knew him.

CAMERON

By four-o'clock, closing time, Cameron decided that the stranger with the pleasant voice wasn't going to show. She'd spent most of the day working in the storage bins, reorganizing and making room for what was left of Lynne Earl's successful show. She needed to get ready for the next one, scheduled next week. Cameron never booked artist's shows back to back like this, but she had no choice. Benjamin Selig, the ninety-year old Pulitzer Prize winning journalist, had offered her his celebrated photographs, plus a collection of old woodcuts he'd acquired during his years in India, with one proviso: the opening must be in September. Normally, she'd close the gallery the last two weeks in September, when things were slow. That's when her only employee, Marsha, took her vacation.

Lynne's show always hung over Labor Day holiday, and normally Cameron would leave it up a little longer, until she closed—not this time. Lynne complained, but Cameron was accustomed to that.

The door opened. A tall, young man walked in, black hair, strong angular features, and the image of all those Patterson males. He wore khaki pants, knit shirt with an emblem on it, and expensive looking loafers.

She jumped to her feet. "You must be Michael." She extended a hand of welcome, and motioned him to pull up a chair. "You're obviously related to the Pattersons."

"My father, but I never knew him. I'm actually looking for medical information about the family."

Cameron sat back and crossed her long, tanned legs. "I thought there was a connection between you and the Melungeon letter I received. You're the one who inquired about Mediterranean diseases."

The color rose in Michael's cheeks. "No, I didn't, but my mother could have contacted them. They must have followed up."

"Why did you come to Hobetown? Most of the Pattersons live in North Carolina."

Michael was prepared for that question, and the lie he would tell. "A woman in the Hartford library said I'd find Patterson graves here. I looked the name up in the phone book and found you. Thought you could help me. Hope you don't mind."

Cameron didn't mind, but this handsome young man wasn't making sense. "There are only three Patterson graves in Hobetown; must be hundreds in North Carolina. Why would anyone send you here? Where was your father born?"

"The Carolinas. My parents weren't married.

He disappeared before I was born."

"What exactly are you looking for?"

Michael hesitated, as if trying to decide what to say. "Most of my life I've had a health problem—fever, pain. None of the doctors my mother took me to could come up with a diagnosis. Said I'd probably outgrow it. There were long periods of time I'd be okay. I hoped the doctors were right, but a few months ago I got really sick. A rheumatologist said I had all the symptoms of Familial Mediterranean Fever, although I didn't appear to be a candidate.

"My grandfather looked up FMF and found Melungeon Cousins. Its members suffered from Mediterranean diseases, and all of them are descendants of a group of early Appalachian settlers called Melungeons. What got Big Mike, my grandfather, stirred up was that his mother came from the same place those Melungeons settled, Newman's Ridge, Tennessee. Both parents have to pass it on. Patterson is a Melungeon name, so we wondered if my father could also be a descendant."

"My husband died seven years ago. There's no Patterson bloodline left in Hobetown. You need to check with the North Carolina family."

"I don't want to take the treatment for FMF if I don't have it," Michael said. "I'm planning on getting married and…."

"If you find out that your father had Melungeon roots then you'll go ahead with the treatment?"

"Yes."

Cameron grimaced. "That is a predicament. My husband's grandparents lived in Duplin County, the eastern part of North Carolina. Most of the Pattersons still live there. We visited one summer and half the county seemed related to them. Sy called the old man 'Chief.' There's a family legend that Chief's mother was Cherokee. But no one ever talked about Melungeons. I suppose...."

Michael leaned forward. "Cherokee? That would connect them to Appalachia, wouldn't it?"

"Guess so. Never thought about it and never heard of the Melungeons. Sy's mother denied the Indian story even though they all have strong Native American features. Like you."

Cameron took her time pulling her shoulder-length blonde hair into a ponytail, and securing it with a rubber band from her desk, trying to understand this handsome young man's quest. Why would he come all the way down here from Connecticut? He could have picked up the phone.

"Guess I got the wrong Carolina." Michael uncrossed his feet, and looked toward the door. "I couldn't get a plane out of Charleston until tomorrow afternoon, so I'm in no hurry. Is there some place I can buy you a drink? Take you to dinner? I'd like to hear more about the Pattersons."

"I've got a better idea, come to my house. I'll show you an album full of men who look just like you. Who knows," she laughed. "One of them might be a relative. Sy had six uncles."

"I don't want to put you to that trouble."

"No trouble. You're family, sorta. I'll fix something. Ever had Lowcountry barbeque?"

"Don't think so."

"Then it's time you did. And you can tell me more about the Melungeons."

When Michael reached the door, he stopped, the smile gone. He leaned against the doorjamb, his body slumped forward. For a moment Cameron feared he was having one of the attacks he'd described, but he straightened up and looked her in the eyes. "I can't go to your house," he said. "I've been misleading you. Can we sit down? I want to explain."

Cameron stared at him, confused. What kind of trick was he pulling? She walked back to her desk. "What's going on?" she demanded.

He pulled an envelope from his pocket and handed it to her. "This is a letter my mother wrote me a few weeks ago. I've been looking at it every day since trying to figure out what to do, trying to decide if I should come down here. You're the only person who can help me."

The envelope was addressed to Michael Duncan at a law firm in Hartford. She opened it and read, looked up at Michael and reread it.

"I don't believe it," Cameron said, rigid with anger. "Sy never said a word about your mother."

Michael handed her a yellowed Polaroid.

"That's my mom, Margaret Duncan."

The photograph was of Sy, wearing a BU sweater, and Hubie Odum, Sy's boyhood friend. Between them a dark-haired girl smiled up at Sy.

"Where was this picture taken?"

"Boston."

She looked carefully at the background. It definitely wasn't Hobetown. Hubie must have been up there visiting Sy for the weekend. 1964. The year before she and Sy were married.

"I didn't want to talk about this on the phone. Felt I had to tell you in person. When I got this letter, my father became a person for the first time. I cannot tell you how that has affected me. I know it's selfish, but I had to come here. And I have to decide about the treatment soon."

Cameron watched him closely, his gestures and expression so like Sy. She couldn't hold back the tears. Of course he was Sy's son.

"Please don't cry," he said. "You'll make me cry."

Cameron laughed through the tears. "I don't know what to say."

"After my doctor's visit, I tried to get information from my mom. You'd have to know her to appreciate what I'm telling you. She runs her life according to astrology and tarot and all sorts of junk like that. I won't go into the details, but Mom insists that my illness had been foretold, and I needed to take the treatment. When she realized I wasn't going to do it if there's a chance my father wasn't a carrier, she sent me this letter. That's why I'm here. Does he have siblings or either parent living?"

"No, just the relatives in North Carolina. I'll give you their addresses."

"I'm sorry about all this. If you like I'll leave."

Cameron picked up the picture. "No you won't! I can't let you walk out of here. Let's go to my place. We need to talk."

Michael left his rented car parked at the gallery and rode with Cameron. During the short drive she tried to fill the awkward space between them by pointing out some of Hobetown's features; the 1737 courthouse with its widows' watch still intact; the one-block business district built along the Greasy River; stores constructed from two-hundred-year-old ballast-stones unloaded off English ships. "Hobetown was an important inland port for colonial Americans. When the timber was cut and the river silted in the channel it was no longer navigable. Hobetown might have disappeared altogether if it hadn't been the county seat.

"See those warehouses?" Cameron pointed to a line of unpainted buildings along the riverfront. "There're built from old growth timbers thicker than a man's body. Used to be where cotton was packed and shipped around the world. Abandoned decades ago and developers are moving in with plans to turn them into shops and condominiums."

"Sounds like you disapprove."

Cameron cocked her head to one side. "Don't suppose I should. But there's something unseemly about outsiders coming in and changing the way we live."

"Is the air always like this? Heavy?" Michael asked, changing the subject. "Feels like I've had a salt rub."

"Humidity, it's worse this time of year."

"Guess you get used to it." He pulled a disagreeable face.

"Like you get used to air pollution in the city?"

Michael grinned. "You got me there."

They drove under ancient live oaks with branches arched across the street.

"This looks a lot like a New England town," he said.

"It's the same period of architecture, but the Ramada's new." Cameron nodded in the distance of a modern stuccoed building. "That's a big deal for Hobetown—first motel."

She pointed to a low brick bunker with a Weyerhauser sign planted in the yard. "Sy worked there. Weyerhauser reclaimed most of the abandoned land when the cotton market collapsed. They planted pine trees for pulpwood. It's what sustains the local population. That and fishing."

"What was his job?"

"Field manager for the southern region. He

died in a boating accident."

"That must have been terrible for you."

"Our daughter was thirteen. It's been real hard for her. She's probably home now."

Michael didn't speak again until they pulled into the driveway. Cameron thought she heard him murmur, "Just like I thought," when he saw her house.

Before she could ask what he meant, Nell burst through the front door and ran across the lawn to meet them, orange hair standing on end. "Got to borrow your car. Give me the keys." She grabbed for Cameron's purse.

Cameron backed off. "What's the matter with yours?"

"Out of gas. Got to meet someone right now. Give 'em to me."

"Nell, I'd like you to meet Michael Duncan, the person who called last night."

Nell looked up, mascara-blackened eyes narrow and suspicious and ran a hand through her spiked hair.

Cameron handed Nell the keys. "Cars don't run on air."

"I know, I know. Got to go."

"I'm heating up barbeque for dinner. Want to join us?"

"Sure. This won't take long." With slow, deliberate steps, Nell walked toward the car. Before she opened the door, she turned and took another look at the stranger.

Cameron and Michael sat on the sofa, looking through an old photo album when Nell slouched through the door.

"Guess I'm a little late," she slurred.

Cameron slumped in her chair at the sound of Nell's voice.

Nell, reeking of marijuana, staggered to a chair and collapsed, arms and legs akimbo. "You still here?" she said to Michael.

"I'll take you back to your car." Cameron looked at Michael and shook her head. No. She wasn't going to tell Nell about Michael now. Nell was in no shape to hear that bombshell.

When they got to the car, Cameron turned to Michael. "I'm sorry about Nell. She's going through a bad time. She recently broke up with her boyfriend, a really nice guy. I was disappointed too." Cameron drew in a breath. "He came home after a stint in the Marines and opened a bar down on the waterfront. Nell helped out. Thought things were finally working out for her."

"My coming here didn't help," Michael said.

"I'll wait 'til you leave to tell her who you are. Can you spend the night? At the Ramada? I'd like to show you around tomorrow morning."

"I guess so."

"I need a chance to work this out."

Michael's eyes told her he understood.

NELL

Nell pawed through the dresser looking for the stash she'd hidden. She'd give it back to Jimmy and cancel some of her debt.

Everything was going wrong in her life and had been since her father died. He was the only person who ever loved her.

Steve said he loved her but that was a lie. If he'd really loved her, he would have forgiven one mistake. It only happened because she'd been smoking dope again. Steve told her that she had to quit, and she mostly did. She knew it made her crazy. Everything was fine between them until just that one time she slipped, just once. She'd run into Cameron's precious Mark at the bar when Cameron had gone to Atlanta. Said he had some amazing grass, and if she didn't tell her mother, he'd share it with her. They walked outside, smoked a joint, and she went home, high and happy. She woke up later with Mark on top of her. It wasn't much of a struggle to get him off. He was so stoned he hardly resisted being pushed out the door. The next day she told Steve, thinking he'd understand and be sympathetic. Confession is good for the soul, they say, but he exploded. Said she was a whore and accused her of coming on to

Mark. How could Steve be so mean to her? She hated him.

And she hated Mark more. She'd wanted everyone to know what a snake he was, but no one believed her; not even her own mother. Nell had tried to warn Cameron about Mark. She'd seen him pick up girls at the bar, and she watched the way he looked at Lynne Earl, Cameron's best friend. That leer had "fuck me" written all over it. But Cameron was too much in love to see. Even crazy Lynne said Cameron was better off without him.

And this Michael guy. There was something really fishy about him, but Cameron couldn't see it. Nell had always been able to spot that in a person. Even Cameron's shrink said she could. He told her that when one part of the brain had experienced trauma, like Fetal Alcohol Syndrome, another part might be heightened. Like a savant. She couldn't recite the calendar backwards or anything like that, but she knew when something wasn't right.

She needed money. Jimmy had threatened to come after her if she didn't pay up for the last grass he'd sold her. She'd given him every cent of her monthly allowance, and she still owed him more. What was she going to do now? She'd have to get it from Cameron somehow.

MICHAEL

A few blocks away Michael checked into the Ramada Inn that smelled of the chemicals used in cheap new furniture, but the room was cool and offered a good view of the river. He collapsed in a chair and stared down at the murky estuary making its lazy way to the sea. Two fishermen were tying a boat to the boardwalk while a tease of squawking seagulls dove after bits of bait the men had thrown across the water.

Hobetown wasn't at all what he'd expected. He thought it would be familiar, the way dreams are when you try to recall them the next day, but nothing was familiar. His mother had driven them here the summer he was six years old. They'd loaded the old station wagon with blankets and pillows, a cooler of luncheon meat, bread and milk, and headed south. Nights were spent at rest stops, stretched out in the back of the wagon in borrowed sleeping bags, fighting mosquitoes, but he didn't mind. It was his first big trip and he was excited about all the new things he saw, until they stopped in Hobetown. His mother parked on a street lined with giant trees where strands of gray moss, like the kind used in haunted houses at Halloween, hung from the branches. She sat silent as a corpse in the hot car, staring at a big white house with a look on her face that scared him. He didn't know why she'd brought him there, and he was afraid to ask. Finally, he crawled in the back seat and went to sleep. When he woke they were on their way to the beach.

Before he'd kept his appointment with Cameron, he'd driven around the five-block residential district looking for that house, but too many looked alike, and he soon gave up. He then drove back along River Road to the business district where he parked the car and walked down the brick sidewalk. None of the buildings he passed was taller than three stories. Many were vacant. Michael supposed that some people would call the town quaint. Not him. It gave him the creeps. He could count on both hands the number of people he passed, including a couple of old men playing checkers in front of a store. Everyone he met spoke or nodded. Life seemed to move in slow motion down here. He wasn't prepared for the heat and humidity, the dense salty air that burned his skin, and the decomposing, organic smell.

The only place to buy something cold to drink was closed, but a guy working inside opened the door and let him in.

"No problem," he told Michael. "What can I get you?"

"Budweiser and a big glass of ice water."

The owner set the beer on the counter. "You from around here?"

"Just passing through."

The man walked to the end of the bar but kept looking over his shoulder, watching him. At the time, Michael thought the scrutiny was because he looked out of place, someone new in town, but now he understood. Everyone in this dump remembered what Sy Patterson looked like.

Michael turned his attention back to the river, imagining a man named Sy Patterson tying his boat to the boardwalk. He might look like the guy, but that was all they had in common. He didn't belong here, and he felt a rush of homesickness. The encounter with drug-crazed Nell, his half-sister, left him feeling sick, but he couldn't blame anyone but himself for the mess he'd caused. He shouldn't have gone home with Cameron—dumb thing to do, but he wanted to know her, and not simply because she was his father's wife. He liked her. Hadn't expected her to be that young looking. Pretty. Funny. Probably the same age as his mother, but didn't look it. Cameron was the kind of woman he'd notice anywhere—smooth blonde hair, bright blue eyes and a friendly smile. He liked the way she looked in her skimpy skirt and tank top that showed off her tan, red toenails poking out of straw sandals. His mother didn't own clothes like that. Cameron was so unlike his mother who took her time warming up to people. He wished he hadn't lied to Cameron about the librarian and Patterson graves in Hobetown, but that was all he could come up with. He'd confess later and she'd probably laugh.

He needed to phone his mother. Yesterday, when he called to say he was going to Hobetown, she'd tried to talk him out of it. His mind was made up, he'd said, and he wanted to know if there was anything else she could tell him about his father. She sounded hurt and took her time before she said that his widow lived on Short Street. He didn't ask how she knew. She'd start her spiel about karma and his destiny. He loved his mother but her preoccupation with his every move drove him crazy, and even now he rarely felt out of range of her patrolling dark eyes. When he was growing up, she'd consult the family's astrological charts before he went off to school each morning. If the signs were auspicious for the aspects, she'd send him loaded with amulets and notes warning the teachers to be on guard. He remembered how he'd wilted with shame when he looked up at recess and saw her at the edge of the schoolyard watching him play. No other mothers did that. He hated it when the kids called her The Spook.

Right now, she'd be sitting in Boston waiting for a call. He hated to disappoint her, but he didn't have the energy. She'd want to know everything Cameron said, and he hadn't decided how much to tell.

But he did have to call Stephanie and reassure her that they'd leave Sunday for their Maine vacation. He'd promised her they'd go shopping tomorrow to pick up things she needed. She was pissed that he'd decided to go to South Carolina instead.

"We still have a whole week," he argued. But Stephanie didn't like anyone changing her plans. He didn't understand why she wouldn't take his problem seriously.

She didn't answer his call. Maybe she'd joined other lawyers from their firm for TGIF half-price drinks at a bar. That meant she'd be out late. He left a message that he'd see her tomorrow.

CAMERON

Cameron left Michael at the Ramada and drove to Lynne Earl's house. She couldn't go home and face Nell. She'd tell her about Michael tomorrow after he left.

Cameron and Lynne had been friends since college. After graduation, Lynne had no home to go to, and Cameron persuaded her to move to Hobetown. She was an ambitious young artist, and if she wanted to paint she needed someone to support her. Out of desperation, she married Hubie Odum, a star-crossed union from the beginning. Since that time, she'd become the gallery's most important artist. Her work was becoming recognized nationally.

Cameron was eager to ask Lynne if Hubie ever spoke of Margaret Duncan. He obviously knew her. But Lynne's car was gone. Cameron turned off the engine and rolled down the windows. This was as good a place as any to think. Sy was two years ahead of Cameron in high school. They'd dated off and on. Nothing serious, but he was the first person she thought of when college vacations came around, and she knew they'd be in Hobetown together. He never mentioned Margaret. Evidently, that relationship was over when he came back home after college. They'd started dating seriously then, and within a year they were married. What would he have done if he'd known Margaret was pregnant? Marry her? Thank God she wanted to keep Michael to herself. But, she grimaced at the thought. If he'd married Margaret he'd still be alive.

When she couldn't stand the mosquitoes any longer she drove home. Nell's bedroom door was open and Cameron stood in the doorway, looking at the mess she'd left. Nell was out of control. Fetal Alcohol Syndrome? Steve? School? She was failing both courses at the Community College. And then yesterday, again, she said she'd like to meet her birth mother. For all the emotion Nell expressed, she might as well have asked if they had any Cokes in the house.

Nell had always known she was adopted. Sy used to tell her that she was luckier than most kids; other parents had to take what they'd been sent, but Nell's parents got to pick her out. She was special. Nell loved to hear him say that, and every so often she'd look up at him with adoring eyes, and ask. "I'm special, aren't I, Daddy?"

It had taken several sessions with their family minister for Cameron to admit that Nell hadn't turned out to be what she expected from the day-old colicky baby they brought home and wanted to love. When Nell was diagnosed with FAS, Sy and Cameron took her to a specialist who suggested they hire a tutor trained to help children with that problem. She did well until puberty shot hormones throughout her tiny body, burning her face with the fire of acne. Nell tried to fend off cruel teasing from other kids but finally she succumbed, too ashamed to leave her room. Not long after that, Sy died. Cameron now realized that she should have sought professional help for both of them. Nell was too fragile to handle the loss of her favorite parent. Grief overwhelmed Cameron, leaving her unresponsive, a poor substitute for the parent Nell lost. Days, weeks, months passed into a blurred memory. It took two years for Cameron to feel her old self again. By that time, Nell had found other comfort.

So long ago, yet an echo of sadness still resounded throughout the house. She'd begun to think that she should sell this place, leave the heartache behind and buy something new, a place with no memories.

Cameron crawled into bed, pulled the cover over her head and closed her eyes. But after a few minutes she knew sleep wasn't possible. She sat up, propped the pillows behind her, and watched the shadows cast by the moon play across the spread. She never got into bed without looking at the empty place beside her. Now she reached out and touched that space, wondering if she really knew who had slept there.

Saturday, September 14

CAMERON

Cameron found Michael waiting by the hotel front door, his hair gleaming wet from the shower. He looked so much like Sy.

"We're going for a little ride," she said. "You ought to know something about your father and his family."

For the next two hours she took him on a tour of the Patterson's brief history in Hobetown, where they'd lived, worked, gone to school, and were buried. Sy had stepped in as mayor upon the death of that town official, and Cameron stopped at the courthouse. She didn't think he'd ever seen a picture of his father except that Polaroid.

On the ground floor of the two hundred year-old building, a room had been dedicated by the preservationist to display historical memorabilia—mostly faded pictures of Hobetown's prosperous days, plus framed land grants and letters from notable men of the colonial period.

Included in the display were photographs and a short biography of distinguished mayors who had served Hobetown. When they got to Sy's picture, Michael stopped. He stared at the photo with such intensity and unconcealed pain in his eyes she feared he would burst out in tears.

Not knowing what to do she said, "Think I'll get a drink of water," and left the room. When she returned, he had moved on to another display and seemed composed.

She enjoyed the curious glances shot their way as she and Michael walked through the courthouse. She wanted people to recognize the handsome young man at her side as a Patterson. She was proud of him, even if he wasn't her son. She avoided mentioning Nell until they drove into the parking lot at the gallery. "I'm really sorry about what happened last night. Nell isn't the monster she appears to be. She's had a lot of problems and being adopted is one of them. Things are particularly sensitive at the moment. She's asked for help to find her birth mother. I don't know what to do."

"It's none of my business, but I'd say help her. I know a little about how that feels."

"I suppose it's normal, wanting to know, but things could be better between us, and it kinda hurts." From the surprised look on Michael's face, Cameron guessed that he was relieved to hear that Nell was adopted.

Michael put his arm around her. "She's a

lucky girl. Couldn't have a better mother."

Cameron grabbed her handbag and walked around the car. "Tour's over, but I've got one more treat before you leave. See that house across the street? We're going there for lunch. Your father was a great admirer of the lady who lives there, Ms. Ernie. She feeds the homeless and sick six days a week. Been doing it for thirty years. She rented her first floor to lawyers a couple of years ago and moved upstairs."

Behind the house, a late model Mercedes Benz was parked on the grass.

"Buford's here," Cameron said. "Ms. Ernie's son."

Cameron and Michael climbed the stairs to a wide covered porch where a rusted freezer dripped a steady trickle of condensation onto the porch below. They tapped on the screen door. Ms. Ernie threw up her hands in greetings, a smile spreading across her plump cheeks. "Come in the house," she said. Her flowered cotton dress, faded from many washings, had resisted the heat and humidity—the starched white collar and cuffs defiantly crisp. She was barely five feet tall beneath a puff of curly, snow-white hair. Hazel eyes shone bright and clear behind her glasses and her soft white skin, always protected from the sun by a floppy straw hat, had a pink, healthy glow.

At the opposite end of the room a large woman wearing a baseball cap set the long oak table with paper napkins and plastic spoons. She looked up, nodded to the newcomers and returned to her work.

"I'd like you to meet a Patterson relative, Michael Duncan from Connecticut." Cameron stepped back.

Ms. Ernie wiped her hands on her apron. "Well, I can certainly tell you're a Patterson. So nice to meet you. Hope you've come for lunch."

"If there's enough," Cameron said.

"Always enough. And Buford's in the living room. Go in and speak to him. Cheer him up." She sidled up to Cameron and whispered, "He's in a bad mood."

Taking Michael's arm, Ms. Ernie steered him to a seat at the table. "Let me fix this young man a glass of tea."

Buford set aside the newspaper and pushed himself out of the chair when Cameron entered the room, an awkward gesture since he'd put on so much weight. His double chin dripped perspireation. Buford would never have been called handsome, but he once had a facial bone structure that gave the appearance of strength. Now that structure had melted. The square jaw slackened, and pasty bags puffed under myopic eyes magnified by thick glasses. Cameron and Buford had grown up together, schoolmates but never friends. He'd been a cruel, sneaky little boy who took items from unlocked houses and blamed black people working in the neighborhood. But he was smart, and he'd become a successful financial investor in Atlanta. She'd rather not bother with him, but Ms. Ernie would be offended if she didn't say hello.

"How you doing, Buford?" Cameron extended her hand.

"Hot as hell." He wiped his face with a rumpled handkerchief. "It's uncivilized to live in this climate without air conditioning." He brushed aside her hand and planted a wet kiss on her cheek. "Come for lunch?" Buford asked, not waiting for a reply. "She's got to stop this. People are complaining. I'm getting letters all the time about what a nuisance she's become. Needs to sell this place and go into a retirement home. I drove down here to talk to her about it."

"Your mother's not a nuisance. She's been here all her life, doing the same thing—ought to be given an award instead of shut down."

"I should know better than to talk to you." He wiped his forehead, again. "I appreciate your concern for my mother, really I do, but I don't think you're being realistic. Things are changing."

"Let's have lunch." Cameron turned and walked back to the dining room.

Michael sat at the table drinking iced tea and looking at an ornately framed painting on the wall.

"Amazing, isn't it?" Cameron said, taking a chair next to him. She looked up at the painting of London from across the Thames. "That's a copy of a Turner. It belonged to Ms. Ernie's father. Back then it was fashionable to have copies of famous paintings."

"I saw a Turner show in Hartford recently. This looks just like one of them."

"It's the best copy I've ever seen," Cameron said.

"You're right about that," Buford said, joining the group. "I keep telling her I'd like to have it to remember my grandfather by."

"Is it valuable?" Michael asked.

"If we knew who copied it, it could be," Cameron replied.

"That's what I keep telling her. Shouldn't be hanging here." Buford threw Ms. Ernie a scowl and walked out on the porch to light a cigarette.

Short Cut Billy, who'd slipped into the room and sat across from Michael, looked up at the painting. "Now, that's what I'd call a picture," he said, with a quick nod of authority at Cameron, an obvious reference to Lynne Earl's impressionistic paintings hanging in the gallery.

As the regulars filed in, Cameron introduced Michael to Mary Sally who had only one arm and one eye; to the Reverend, who thanked Jesus with every breath for everything that came to mind; to Mr. Roy Williams, with no teeth and milky eyes scabbed with cataracts.

Michael, his eyes wide and playful, watched the coterie arrive and take their place at the table. Every so often he smiled at Cameron, as he listened to the conversation among the guests.

When they returned to the gallery, Nell sat

on the steps, waiting. She'd washed the color out of her hair, and except for the black lipstick and studs and loops, Cameron thought she looked pretty.

"I've been trying to find you all morning. Why'd you take him to that rat hole?" she stuck her tongue out, and waggled her head. Cameron understood Nell's awkward attempt to be funny—making amends for her behavior of the night before.

Just then Buford called from across the street. "I want to stop by before I leave."

Cameron waved and nodded.

Michael turned to Cameron. "I've got to get going or I'll miss my plane. I can't thank you enough." He started to say more, but his voice caught in his throat.

Cameron hugged him goodbye. "Let me know if you find out anything from the North Carolina relatives. I'll try to make some inquiries too. She watched him drive down Sunset Avenue.

Nell turned her back and walked away.

"Wait a minute." Cameron called out to her to come back. "We need to talk."

MICHAEL

Michael drove the two-lane road to the airport through a tunnel of shadows cast by mammoth overhanging trees. He passed unpainted houses, jacked-up on pilings, with black children playing in the yards, but he saw little of it. His mind was on his father and the mixed race Melungeons. Now he knew. The Indian grandmother clinched it. In the seventeen hundreds the Melungeons migrated from Virginia down to North Carolina and joined a tribe of Native Americans called Lumbees. After sixty years, most of the Melungeons moved on to Tennessee, leaving their genes behind. He was sure the Indian grandmother was a descendant of those who remained. That's how the gene was introduced to the Pattersons.

From what he'd read, these people were ostracized wherever they settled. As the first white settlers in the Appalachians, they interbred with the Indians and escaped black slaves. They called themselves Portygees. Historical records describe them as a mean, thieving lot who'd shoot any man seen trespassing on their property. Deprived of public education and the vote, they banned together in settlements staying ahead of the encroaching white men.

Interest in the Melungeons had been revived with Wayne Winkler's book *Walking Toward the Sunset*. Big Mike had ordered it and passed it on to Michael. It portrayed a more realistic, kinder picture of these forgotten people. Michael wasn't sure how he felt about being a descendant, but then, after a few generations, who knew anyone's true origin?

Stephanie had dismissed the subject as folkloric nonsense. But how was she going to feel if the side effects that the doctor spoke of kicked in? Did she care enough to stick with him? Did he care enough to put her through it?

Their relationship had happened so fast he felt he'd been hit with a runaway truck. On his first day at work with the law firm she'd walked in his office and introduced herself as the boss's daughter. Would he like to have a drink after work? He was flattered and impressed with the tall, beautiful lawyer. Hooking up with her seemed the right thing to do. He hadn't minded being swept into her privileged world.

CAMERON

After Michael drove away, Cameron asked Nell to come inside the gallery. They needed to talk.

Nell sat quietly, her expression changing from anger to disbelief. Cameron didn't show her the letter from Michael's mother. Maybe one day she would, but not now. Nell didn't ask to read it.

"It's a lie," Nell said. "Do you believe him?"

"I believe he's your father's son."

"Why is he turning up now?"

"Like he said, he wants to know if the Pattersons had any of these diseases."

"That's a crock. He could find that out without coming down here. He's after something."

"We need to put it behind us. We'll probably never see him again."

"I hope not." Nell gripped the arms of the chair. "He's up to something." Nell closed her eyes and slumped in the chair. "I hate him."

"Michael?"

"All men."

We don't know the story, Nell. We never will. But we do know that your father loved us."

"Yeah? I wonder who else he loved."

Cameron took a deep breath and walked toward the back door. She had to get out. In a voice straining to hold her anger in check, she said, "I need to go home and change. Watch the gallery for a few minutes. I won't be long."

"Why are you changing?"

"I'm trying to see Dr. Rao after I close."

"You dress up for your shrink?"

"I'm not dressing up. I just want to put on something fresh."

Nell settled back in the chair and tilted her head to the side. "Sure you don't have a crush on that guy?"

*

When Cameron returned to the gallery, she found Buford and Nell huddled in a conversation that ended abruptly when they saw her coming through the back door. Nell left immediately.

Buford walked around the gallery, stopping briefly at each painting. "I don't want you to think I'm not appreciative of what you do for my mother," he said. "But it's time for her to stop. She's almost ninety. Those people aren't going to starve if she doesn't feed them."

"How do you know?"

"Come on, Cameron, there's all kinds of agencies to feed people like that."

"Name one around here."

Red splotches blossomed on his cheeks, his

blood pressure likely ratcheted up a few points. He coughed and dislodged a chest of asthmatic phlegm. "You don't help the dregs of society by giving them a handout," he said, spitting into his handkerchief.

"I'm not about to help any group that wants to put your mother on the street. Forget it, Buford."

"That's not what I wanted to talk to you about. I've made a reservation at the Ramada for my mother in case the hurricane hits. Would you make sure she goes? You know how stubborn she is."

"Of course I will." She resisted asking why he couldn't take care of his own mother. She was ready to tell him goodbye when he pointed to a painting across the room.

"This Lynne Earl stuff is pretty good. How much you take for that one?"

"The price is on it."

"It's not on the same level with other works in my collection, but I can find some place for it." He reached in his pocket for his wallet, and tossed his credit card on the desk.

When Buford left, Cameron picked up the phone and called Lynne. "I just sold another painting. Two thousand dollars, cash."

A loud whoop blasted from the phone. "Couldn't come at a better time. I'm sitting here looking at a stack of bills."

"Tell me you won't spend any of it on your deadbeat boyfriend's schemes."

"No way. I'm going to see a money manager next week and get myself on a budget. No more investments."

"Why don't I believe you?"

"Because you know me. I'm just a sex addict, can't resist those young guys."

"Sex is no excuse to ruin your life."

"That's easy for you to say."

"What do you mean?" Cameron knew exactly what she meant. There had only been one man she'd slept with since Sy's death. No telling how many Lynne had enticed into her bed.

Lynne chuckled. "Sorry. Don't be so touchy. Let's have dinner tonight and celebrate."

"I'm trying to see my psychiatrist after work, if I can get him."

"It's Saturday. What's wrong?"

"Everything."

"That's not good. Let's meet afterwards at the cafe

Since Nell's breakup with Steve, Cameron had avoided going there. "How about someplace else?"

"Come on, Cameron. It's not your fault Steve and Nell had a falling-out. Get over it. Nell has. She's there all the time. Besides, there's no place else to go."

"Nell wants to upset Steve. I don't."

"Whatever. Meet me there at eight."

The fact that Nell went there was another

reason not to go. Eventually Steve would tire of seeing her plopped down at the end of the bar flirting with every guy who came in, and there'd be a scene.

Cameron hung up and flipped the phone index to Dr. Rao's number. She'd survived the loss of both parents, the death of her husband, and the disappointment of an unloving daughter without the need for psychiatric treatment, but Mark's departure had left her devastated. Dr. Rao called it collateral damage. He'd prescribed once-a-week visits, then every other week and at their last session asked how she felt about once a month. "It's almost graduation time," she'd joked.

She needed to talk to someone besides Lynne. She couldn't get the Polaroid off her mind. She left her name and number with the answering service. Thirty minutes later Dr. Rao called. "What's going on?" he asked, in his unmistakable Indian accent.

"I'm not ready for graduation." She tried to sound humorous, not desperate. "I need to see you before Tuesday. It's kind of an emergency."

He didn't ask why, and she didn't feel compelled to explain. Mutual trust was one of the unexpected benefits of therapy. They agreed on five forty-five.

His office was in the next town, thirty miles away. Hobetown didn't have a psychiatrist. Initially, she'd been reluctant to make an appointment with a doctor named Sanjay Rao. She couldn't imagine how he'd understand someone like her, but talking to him turned out to be the easiest thing she'd ever done. And it didn't hurt that he looked like a Bollywood movie star - his black hair combed flat against his head, straight and shining except for the curls around his ears that refused to be disciplined.

She wanted to know everything about the dark stranger from halfway around the world, with eyes that could catch fire one minute and melt with compassion the next. She'd never known anyone from India, an exotic place she'd only read of. So far, she hadn't mustered the courage to ask personal questions. She only knew that he'd been born in Delhi and trained at Johns Hopkins.

When she put the phone down she felt she'd been thrown a lifeline. Just hearing his voice calmed her. All morning she'd struggled to appear at ease with Michael, when half the time she felt she'd burst into tears. Had she known it would be so painful, she wouldn't have insisted they do the tour. She'd never forget the look on his face when he saw his father's picture hanging in the courthouse with the governor's award beside it.

* * *

Dr. Rao pushed his chair away from the desk and crossed his arms. He wore a dark gabardine jacket and spotless white shirt, which seemed even whiter against his bronzed neck. Cameron admired the smooth skin stretched over a face clearly defined by near-perfect features—narrow eyebrows arched above almond-shaped dark eyes, thin nose, and mouth that turned up slightly at the corners, like the serene smile on the bodhisattva watching over his office from the corner of the room.

She started to comment on his lustrous pink silk tie. It made her think of an elongated tongue. What would he make of that? What did she make of it? She'd never seen him wear anything but conservative ties, and she felt like saying that he should dress like this more often.

He listened to Cameron describe Michael and the scene with Nell, nodding and taking notes. "Let's back up a minute," he said, when she ran out of words. "What you've told me about Michael Duncan opens a whole new set of problems. Let's talk about the unfinished business from your last visit before we tackle this. Last week we talked about you getting in touch with Nell's mother. Have you done anything about that?"

"I looked up her grandparents in the phone book. They still live in Back Creek. She mentioned her birth mother again yesterday."

"Can you think of any reason why?"

The question surprised Cameron. "She wants to meet her biological mother? What else?"

"Has Michael Duncan's appearance changed your plans?"

"It's confused me. If I arrange a meeting between Nell and her mother now, will she think I'm trying to get rid of her."

"Are you?"

"Of course not. I love my daughter. I wish she loved me."

"You don't think she does?"

She'd come to talk about Michael, not the same unresolved problems with Nell. She looked out the window before she said what seemed so obvious. "If she loved me, why would she act like this?"

Dr. Rao leaned across the desk, forcing Cameron to meet his gaze. "We hurt people we love all the time. Don't we?"

Cameron closed her eyes, and took a deep breath. "I hate to admit it, but I've known Michael less than twenty-four hours, and I feel closer to him than I do to Nell."

"And it would be natural for you to look at Michael and wish your adopted child had turned out like him."

Cameron bristled. "That's an awful thing to say." She was near tears. "Nell's my child."

"I know," Dr. Rao soothed. "But it's best to get these feelings of guilt on the table so they can be dealt with. Your attachment to Michael is normal."

Cameron turned away and looked at the bodhisattva, a calming presence in a room filled with so much angst.

"Do you intend to talk to Nell's grandmother?" he asked.

"Michael thinks I should. Do you?"

"Let's talk about it again on Tuesday. In the meantime, I suggest you spend time with Nell. She has every right to feel threatened by this intruder. She must be thinking if this is the prodigal son, who am I? Michael is a terrible shock for both of you."

As he spoke he pushed loose paper clips into a circle. "You're going through an extremely stressful time. It's unfortunate that these events have collided, but Cameron I think you're stronger than you were six months ago and more able to handle them. What do you think?"

"I might be stronger, but you're not going to get rid of me any time soon."

"I don't want to get rid of you. Far from it." His face flushed, and he quickly reached for the desk calendar, avoiding her eyes.

Cameron didn't miss her stoic therapist's moment of unease. "You're right. I am stronger. Six months ago I couldn't have talked about any of this rationally."

She rose to leave, but he held up his hand.

"The relationship with Nell will never be healed until the two of you can talk about Mark. I could schedule another appointment for the three of us, if she's willing."

Cameron flinched. "Not now." She wasn't going to risk another scene like the last and only time the three of them had met. Dr. Rao had arranged a meeting in the hopes of establishing better communication between mother and daughter. It went well until Cameron asked Dr. Rao if Nell could have misunderstood what had happened between her and Mark. Nell exploded. "Don't you think I know when someone tries to rape me? Just because I have FAS, I'm not retarded." She jumped to her feet and shouted at Cameron. "Mark is a snake and you're blind," then ran crying from the room.

Cameron realized how it must have sounded to Nell; her mother chose to believe Mark rather than her own daughter. Later, she tried to explain, but Nell wouldn't listen.

Cameron looked toward the door, ready to leave. "Nell will never admit that Mark wasn't trying to have sex with her."

He didn't comment.

"If it wasn't for Nell, we'd be together," she added, as an afterthought.

"If it wasn't for Mark, you and Nell wouldn't have this problem." Dr. Roa replied.

LYNNE

Lynne waited at the crowded bar seated next to Dallas Rigsbee, Hobetown's police chief. She wore a short jean skirt and low-cut, tight tee shirt with "Expose Yourself to Art" stretched over her full breasts. Her long red hair fell across her shoulders and down her back. She handled herself like a woman who knew how good she looked and enjoyed making the most of it. All along the bar, young guys glanced her way and smiled. But none would approach as long as the police chief had her attention.

Dallas's hand was on her thigh. When he saw Cameron enter the bar he rose from his stool and backed away, hiking his pants under his extended belly. "Guess it's time for me to be leaving," he drawled.

Strands of body hair poked through the gap in his shirt. Cameron looked away and spoke to Steve who nodded toward an empty booth.

"Thanks for the drink." Lynne called out to Dallas.

Why do you talk to that cretin?" Cameron snapped.

"Stay on his good side."

"What good side?"

"I don't blame you for hating him. But it doesn't do you any good, Cameron. He could hurt you."

"He already has, remember? He nearly raped me."

"I know he did, but that was a long time ago. You need to get over it. Do you know he plans to run for sheriff? Probably win."

"You're not going out with him again, are you?"

"Of course not. I've got all I can handle with Buddy. Besides, Dallas is too old."

"Yeah. He's our age."

Lynne wasn't going to let Cameron's hatred of Dallas dampen the effects of a couple gin and tonics. She sat back, grinning, and flipped her long hair toward the boys at the end of the bar. "Aren't we in a pissy mood."

"I don't care who you sleep with, even if he is the same age as Nell. I just remember how depressed you were when that last guy skipped town and left you with maxed-out credit cards."

"Buddy's different. He just got a job as assistant manager at the Ramada. He can take care of himself."

"I hope so. He's been living off you long enough." Cameron pushed an envelope across the table. "In the meantime, here's a check for the painting, less the commission. Go on that cruise you talked about and find a nice guy."

Lynne leaned forward and smacked Cameron a kiss. "I love you. You're the best friend anyone could have, but I hate to disappoint you- nice guys aren't attracted to me like they are to you."

Cameron lifted an eyebrow. "All one of them?"

"You could have had plenty of guys if you weren't so choosy."

"So could you if you were a little choosier."

Lynne laughed. "Maybe so, but you're better off without Mark." Seeing the frown on Cameron's face she quickly added. "What the hell is bugging you?"

Cameron sloughed into the corner of the booth and stared hard at her friend. "I can't believe you keep saying that about Mark."

"Okay, I'll stop. Now, tell me. What sent you flying to the shrink this afternoon?" She lowered her voice. "Nell?"

"This isn't about Nell, but Dr. Rao did say she and I had to talk about Mark. He said its possible she could have convinced herself that he really tried to rape her. People with FAS sometimes suffer from delusions."

"Bullshit." Lynne slapped the table. "Nell's not delusional. She's a pain in the ass, and spoiled rotten, but she's as sharp as anyone I know. The minute you and Sy heard the term FAS you decided she was a victim. There's nothing the matter with that girl except she's dyslectic, just like I am, and a zillion other successful people."

"Nell wants to meet her mother. Out of nowhere, she comes up with that."

Lynne's mouth dropped. "You know where her mother is?"

"I think I can find her."

"You should. Do Nell good to meet that little chippie. Make her appreciate what a good deal she got."

"I don't know whether to believe her or not. Maybe she's just trying to get attention."

Lynne sat back, thoughtful. "What does Dr. Rao say about the Dallas incident? Maybe that's gotten mixed up in this problem with Nell."

"I've never talked about it."

"What! You've been seeing him for six months and never told him about nearly getting raped? What's wrong with you?"

Cameron covered her eyes with her hand. "It doesn't have anything to do with Mark."

"Jesus Christ, Cameron. I can't believe you. It has everything to do with Mark. You refuse to accept that what happened to you could happen to your daughter—and with the guy you're in love with. Admit it. You don't want to believe it, and it's messing with your head." Lynne reached across the table and squeezed Cameron's arm. "I understand why you're upset. I'm sorry I picked on you."

Cameron took a sip of her drink and looked

over at Steve who'd been glancing at the two women every few minutes. "But that's not what sent me flying to Dr. Rao."

*

When they reached the parking lot Lynne's car wouldn't start. Cameron said she'd take her home. They rode in silence—Lynne remembering those years so long ago when she'd come home with Cameron from college, a home so different from hers. Cameron's parents, quiet, dignified people, taught at the community college. Their home, which Cameron still lived in, with its comfortable old furniture and books, was a refuge. When you opened the front door, you could count on a delicious aroma coming from the sun-filled kitchen, where the family gathered to eat and discuss subjects never brought up in her home. She'd fallen in love with the forgotten little river town nesting in the middle of salt marshes. She'd sit for hours by the lagoon watching golden sea grasses sway in the heavy coastal breezes. Elegant, long-legged herons tiptoed through the shallows in search of prey. She loved sketching the craggy fishermen, bent from years of hauling nets, the ancient fish house where the day's catch was weighed and sold, and the shrimp packers, mostly black people whose skin shone like polished stone. She loved the languid river threading its way among wetlands, the humidity so thick in summer it hung in the air and reshaped the world in misty grays.

After graduation, Lynne moved to Hobetown, the only home she knew. Lynne's father had remarried and started another family. Lynne's mother lost her battle with alcohol and disappeared into the abyss of addiction.

"You're awfully quiet," Cameron said, drawing Lynne back to the present.

Lynne rolled down the car window and reached in her bag for a cigarette. "I was thinking about your parents and how good they were to me. They saved my life."

"We were so young and vulnerable." Lynne paused and closed her eyes. "My awful parents. My miserable marriage to Hubie. Your parents dying of cancer the same year. Sy's senseless death. We've had more than our share of misery."

"Hobetown hasn't been very good to us. I know why I stayed. Why did you?" Cameron asked.

Lynne took a drag on the cigarette then flipped it out the window. "'Cause I didn't have any place to go. Besides, I love it. You don't have to be born in a place to belong." The question annoyed her. She knew Cameron wasn't suggesting that she was an outsider, but that's how it felt.

"I take it back," Cameron said. "Hobetown has been very good to you, at least professionally."

"It's about time. I've been working my ass off for twenty years."

Lynne looked at her best friend, the only person in the world who understood her. Cameron had always been the strong one, even when faced with tragedy, but tonight Lynne saw something that hadn't been there before. Doubt?

"Don't let this Michael stuff get you down," Lynne said. "Sy was devoted to you."

"I used to think so. Maybe there were other women."

"You would have known."

"I didn't know about Michael's mother."

"He didn't either." Lynne's voice pitched higher. "Besides, that was before you. Get over it. Be glad you had a husband who loved you. And it's time to get over Mark. Other guys are out there."

Cameron smiled. "Speaking of, I think my psychiatrist made a pass at me this afternoon."

"You think?"

"I think he thought he was, but he wasn't."

"What the hell are you talking about, Cameron?"

"I guess he was, but he's my doctor."

"You must have liked it. He's Indian, isn't he? Tell me about him?"

"That's all I know except he's really sexy and has gorgeous eyes."

"Aren't you supposed to fall in love with your therapist? Part of the treatment?"

Cameron stopped the car in front of Lynne's

house, a four-room bungalow, formerly occupied by a family who raised carnivorous plants. She'd turned their greenhouse into a studio.

Lynne got out and took a few steps before turning around, then motioned for Cameron to roll down the window. "Don't fuck him yet," she said, loud enough for the neighbors across the road to hear. "A good shrink's hard to find."

CAMERON

Cameron got home a little past ten, exhausted, determined to be bathed, in bed and asleep before eleven. She wanted to put this night behind her. Being that close to Dallas brought back all the hate she'd borne him since that night seven years ago. Seeing the smirk on his face, his hand working its way up Lynne's thigh, and those wet lips left her sick.

Lynne was right to be shocked that she'd never told Dr. Rao about Dallas. Was she afraid to talk about it? Let the genie out of the bottle? What else would come spilling over? Had she really started therapy because Mark walked out, or because she felt guilty that she'd brought him into the house and he tried to have sex with her daughter?

She lay across the bed waiting for the tub to fill, and wishing she could erase the memory of the night Dallas had almost raped her. It stuck in her brain like a tune that played over and over. It had happened less than three months after Sy's death. Nell had a sleepover at a friend's house, and Lynne talked Cameron into going to the Saturday night dance at the country club. "You need to get out of this house," Lynne had said. "Your friends want to see you."

She hadn't stayed long and was looking for a ride home when Dallas said he'd be glad to drop her off. She didn't think anything of it when he turned the motor off and walked her to the door. Before she could tell him good night he pushed her inside, all the while trying to kiss her mouth and neck, grabbing her breasts.

She struggled to get away, beating him with her fists, and yelling for him to stop. But he kept pushing and dragging her into the house, to the sofa, where he rolled on top of her and tried to pull off her clothes. She cringed remembering his wet mouth all over her face, and his voice, slurred with alcohol, telling her that since Sy was gone, he'd take care of her. With one hand he held her arms above her head and with the other, worked at his zipper.

He would have raped her if headlights from a car turning into her driveway hadn't stopped him. Dallas shifted just enough to allow her to get out from under him and run out the door and down the steps. Hubie Odum was coming up the walk.

"You left your billfold at the club," Hubie said. "Thought I better drop it off before you missed it." He stopped. "What's wrong?"

She grabbed his arm. "Dallas. He's inside." Hubie tried to put his arm around her, but Cameron sunk to the ground and began sobbing. "He tried to rape me."

Before Hubie could reach the door, Dallas calmly walked down the steps and looked at Cameron, crumpled on the ground. "Don't know what's wrong with her. We've been trying to cheer her up all evening."

Hubie grabbed Dallas by the shirt. "You low-life son-of-a bitch."

Dallas turned his head and spat on the ground. "How you doing, Hubie?" He walked to his car and drove away.

Cameron was too ashamed to talk about what had happened She only told Lynne who already knew. Dallas had given her his version of the incident.

"If I were you, I'd forget it," Lynne had responded. "Dallas is a fool when he's drinking and dangerous when he's not."

But she hadn't forgotten it and never would.

Sunday, September 15

MICHAEL

Michael returned home to find a message from Stephanie. She'd gone to the shore and wouldn't be back until late. She'd see him tomorrow. The trip had exhausted him, and he didn't mind crashing at his place—alone.

Sunday morning he got up early, but waited till nine to call. Stephanie answered the phone, half asleep.

"You don't sound very happy to hear from me," he said.

She moaned and said to call back later.

No need to hurry, he thought. He'd give her a little longer before he went over and pulled her out of bed.

One of his buddies had called Stephanie "high maintenance." Michael had to agree. She was also smart, savvy, rich, and swung the door to her father's law firm wide open for him. Already her family treated him like one of them. There were problems, but weren't there always?

On his way to her apartment, Michael stopped at the convenience store and picked up bagels, cream cheese and the New York Times. He fumbled for change to pay the young woman at the counter, who smiled at him, but Michael never looked up. His mind was on Hobetown and how much he would tell his mother about the visit. He hadn't called her yet. She'd be upset that he'd gone home with Cameron, and he'd decided not to tell that part. He didn't like to lie, but it was best to say that he'd only talked to Cameron for a few minutes and saw no reason to ever see her again. He'd call his mother tonight, after he got the story straight in his head.

When Stephanie let him in, he tried to kiss her, but she pushed him away and backed off.

"Morning breath," she protested, and raised her hand to her mouth. She had on a tee shirt he didn't recognize.

The sour stench of alcohol clung to her.

"You must have had quite a night." He wrinkled his nose and turned away. She looked terrible. "Get in the shower, and I'll make coffee."

She brushed him aside and fell back in bed.

Michael put on a pot of coffee. While he waited for it to brew he glanced at the sports section of the newspaper.

He poured two cups, adding extra cream and sugar to hers, and carried it to the bed. "Come on, princess. You can't stay there all day."

He leaned over to kiss her and his eye caught the glitter of a foil wrapper under the bed. Condom wrapper. They didn't use condoms. She was on the pill. She opened her eyes and saw the torn pack in his hand.

"What's this?" Michael asked. "What's going on?"

She grabbed it from him. "Nothing. Forget it."

"What do you mean nothing? It's a goddamn condom. Who's been here?"

Stephanie threw the covers aside and bolted out of bed. "For Christ's sake, Michael. You come over here, wake me up, and start yelling. Leave me alone." She stomped into the bathroom and slammed the door.

Stephanie was a party girl and loved to flirt, but he never thought she'd do this. There was only one explanation. How could she do that to him? He picked up her pillow and threw it across the room. "Bitch," he yelled, and walked out the door.

*

Stephanie called three times, but he didn't answer the phone, he didn't need her explanation of what had happened. One of the messages she left said she'd had too much to drink. It had nothing to do with him. She was ready to go to Maine. She didn't sound contrite, just matter of fact. At least she hadn't lied. He didn't expect her to grovel, but he thought she'd be a little remorseful.

He spent the rest of the day doing laundry and watching a golf tournament on TV. Anything to take his mind off Stephanie. But the seed of doubt was planted. How could he marry a woman who cheated on him when he was out of town for one night? And to hell with taking her to Maine.

By late afternoon he needed to get outside, away from the phone and the closeness of his small apartment. He changed into sweat clothes and headed for the park. After thirty minutes of laps he stopped and bought a bag of popcorn to feed the pigeons. A woman and her toddler joined him on his bench, and he shared the popcorn with the little boy, who squealed in delight each time the pigeons fluttered near. The sky was almost dark when he walked back home.

He cooked a hamburger and sat down to watch news of the hurricane they were calling Hilda that people had talked about during his short visit to Hobetown. It had slowed down, gaining strength. On its present course it would hit the U. S. coast next weekend. Those people down there lived with the threat of hurricanes and knew what to do, but it made him anxious thinking about it.

Later, he called his grandfather and told him about Hobetown.

"Sounds like it got you down," Big Mike said.

"It's not the trip. I came home feeling good, but things have gone to hell here."

"Something the matter at the firm?"

"No, it's Stephanie. Don't tell Mom."

"Don't tell Mom what?"

"I'm gone one night and come home to find she's been with another guy."

"Don't worry about me telling her that."

"We're supposed to be getting married."

"Well, girls are more independent than they used to be."

"Bullshit."

Big Mike chuckled. "Don't do anything foolish."

"I know what you're thinking. Stephanie's the door to success."

"You're half right. She can open doors, but I wouldn't expect you to let any woman make a fool out of you. Just think about what you're doing before you fly off the handle."

"I'd planned to take off next week. Steff and I were going to Maine, fishing. Think I'll still go. Want to come along?"

"Thought you had a job."

"Vacation. I've been booking over sixty hours a week for the last six months. It's time for a break."

"What about Stephanie?"

"She was only going to humor me. Fishing's not her thing."

"That's mighty tempting, but I've got a better idea. This Melungeon stuff's got me all stirred up. Been doing some research. Thought I'd go down to Newman's Ridge this week and see where my mother was raised. Come go with me."

"When?"

"Tuesday. Fly down to Atlanta and pick up a car. The mountains should be pretty this time of year. You can learn something about your ancestors."

Right then Michael's Tennessee ancestors didn't interest him, but he liked the idea of spending a few days with his grandfather. "Sure you hadn't rather go fishing?"

"I've arranged with the lady who writes all that stuff about the Melungeons to take me on a tour. Already sent her a check. Thought I'd surprise you with what I found out. But this is better because I won't have to spend too much time with the old lady."

Michael hung up and called Steff's number. He hoped she wasn't home, and he'd leave a message, but she answered.

"I've been calling you all afternoon," she snapped.

"I didn't want to talk to you."

"Don't be ridiculous. I told you I had too much to drink. I guess you never make a mistake."

"Not like that. I'd never cheat on you, Stephanie."

"This is getting tiresome. I'm going to hang up. Call me when you're reasonable."

"Hang on a minute. I've decided to call off the fishing trip. I'm going to Tennessee with my grandfather."

"What! You can't do that. I'm ready to go to Maine."

"If I thought you really wanted to sit in a cabin in the woods and get eaten up with mosquitoes I'd feel bad."

"We don't have to go to Maine."

"I think it's better if you and I don't see each other for a few days."

Michael could hear her short, angry breaths. Several moments passed before she spoke. "If you think I give a damn what you do, you're crazy. You can go to hell, as far as I'm concerned."

MARGARET DUNCAN

Margaret and Big Mike bought a duplex in their neighborhood when Michael was nine years old. Big Mike said they'd outgrown his two-bedroom home, even though Margaret insisted she didn't mind sharing a room with her son.

Big Mike scratched a garden patch in the back yard and Margaret planted flowers along the front walk. The garage became Big Mike's tool shop, and a safe place for Michael to lock up his new bike. To pay her share of the mortgage Margaret took a receptionist's job in a doctor's office. Michael was a happy little boy, content to stay close to her and his grandfather. She remembered those as the best years. They had gone by too fast.

She only worked part-time now. Michael told her she should stop altogether, but she liked the idea of adding to her Social Security. Someday she'd need that money. She'd take her grandchildren, the ones Michael and Stephanie would have, and show them the world, something she couldn't afford to do with Michael.

She'd been waiting for Michael's call and grabbed the phone on the first ring. "How'd it go?"

she asked, trying not to betray the anxiety that had gripped her since he left for Hobetown. She'd had compatibility charts drawn for the relationship between Michael and Hobetown, and each one showed danger for Michael, all connected to Cameron Patterson. If it hadn't been for that woman she and Sy would have gotten married and their destinies would have been fulfilled. Michael wouldn't listen to her when she tried to explain the astrological readings; he even scoffed. He was such a sentimental boy. It would be just like him to go down there and fall in love with the place and want to go back. She'd devoted her life to him, and she didn't intend to share him with anyone in Hobetown. The fear of Sy's wife might sound silly to people who didn't understand astrology, but Margaret knew she was a threat.

"Did you meet his wife?" she asked.

"I stopped by her gallery. She wasn't able to help much. Told me to try North Carolina. Drove around Hobetown and went to the courthouse. It's a strange little town."

"What are you going to do now?"

"Think I'll go ahead with the treatment. It's likely the North Carolina Pattersons have Melungeon ancestors."

"Michael, you didn't have to go the South Carolina to find that out." "I know, Mom."

"Forget about Hobetown. There's nothing down there for you."

Margaret felt a little better after they hung up. At least this trip had encouraged him to start the medication. Everything she read about FMF said that in a few years they'd isolate the gene and have a better treatment, but it wouldn't hurt to get a head start.

When he drove around Hobetown, had he gone past the Patterson's place? She'd lived much of her life dreaming about it, fantasizing how it would feel to live there, to be the woman who planted the flowers, raised the children, and cooked the meals for the man she loved. Shortly after Michael's sixth birthday she'd succumbed to her obsession and driven the two of them to South Carolina. She told Big Mike that she'd gotten a special deal at one of those island resorts. She hadn't lied; they did go to an ocean side motel after their detour and had a wonderful time.

Had she known he'd go to Hobetown, she'd never have written the letter. But he was so upset with her when he left that morning that she knew things would never be right between them until she told him the truth about his father. After he called and said he was going down there, she phoned the Metaphysical Center for an appointment. She was too nervous to drive, so Big Mike reluctantly agreed to take her. The psychic reader at the center immediately saw danger. When he added Friday the thirteenth to the mix, and an ominous astrological conjunction, she was sure Michael was in danger. She'd hardly slept these last two nights worrying about it.

Visions filtered through her dreams sending warnings that lay in the back of her mind. She didn't understand their meaning. She kept dreaming of water and smoke, a burning hot sun and she'd wake up weak with fear. And she heard voices. Warnings, all around her, warning voices. One thing she did understand was that she wanted Michael to stay away from Hobetown and that Patterson woman.

Now that he knew about his father she'd tell him the rest of the story the next time they were together. How she'd had her astrological chart read a few days before she met Sy. The reader had said, "A man will come into your life very soon who will fulfill your karma. You will recognize him, and your life will be transformed." Then Sy Patterson walked into the neighborhood bar where she and friends gathered. They were together constantly for the next year. She spent most weekends at his apartment. He never asked her to go to South Carolina with him, and she didn't press. After he finished school and they were married, there'd be plenty of time for that. They didn't talk about the future. The present was enough.

As graduation neared, Sy became indifferent, making excuses not to be with her. She hoped it was just the pressure of finishing school and being on his own. His easy-going mood turned sour. He gave up his apartment and moved in with friends. Most weekends he went home to Hobetown. She asked what was wrong, but he responded half-heartedly, saying he had a lot on his mind. Finally he called and said they had to talk. Could she meet him at the park? When she saw him sitting on a bench, and he turned his face toward her, she knew what to expect. He told her he'd resumed his relationship with his high school sweetheart, Cameron. She'd just finished college and returned to Hobetown. He wanted to be honest. He was sorry to hurt her, but he hoped to marry Cameron. She didn't tell him she'd just found out she was pregnant. Maybe she could have made him marry her, but what good would that have done? He'd always be thinking about the woman he really loved. She decided then that she'd go home. Her father would understand and welcome her.

    When she went back to the astrologer the next day, crying, he said that the highest calling was to live one's karma, not to question. Never look back. That's exactly what she did.

    Now that Michael was back safe, she felt a weight had been lifted from her heart. It reaffirmed that they had lived according to their karma just as it had been revealed in the past life regression. It didn't matter that Michael refused to accept it. It didn't change anything.

    She reached under the bed and pulled out a

thick scrapbook of clippings she'd collected from the Hobetown newspaper. For twenty-four years she'd subscribed to the biweekly and cut out every reference about Sy Patterson. There were plenty. She'd written the courthouse and obtained transscripts when Sy was mayor. She knew about his commendations and about his promotions with Weyerhauser. Knew when he and Cameron went to parties, had parties, chaired political rallies and fundraisers. Knew when he died and where he was buried. This book told everything about his short stay on earth, except his purpose for being here. She'd give it to Michael someday.

Monday, September 16

CAMERON

Cameron woke early Monday morning and lay in bed listening to the chirping, croaking and buzzing songs coming from the garden. All of God's tiny creatures were busy at work. She'd spent the previous day out there among them, moving flowerpots to the garage, checking the trees for dead limbs and clearing the spent flowerbeds in preparation for the storm.

Nell hadn't come home Saturday night, and all weekend Cameron had the place to herself. It gave her time to recover from Michael's visit without having to explain or argue with Nell about his motives. She understood why he felt compelled to come to Hobetown, was glad he did and hoped he'd come back.

The gallery was closed on Mondays, so this was a good time to drive to Back Creek and visit Thelma Poteat, Nell's grandmother. The address in the phone book was #8 Ponderosa Mobile Park. That shouldn't be hard to find.

THELMA

Back Creek, once a thriving community of fishermen ten miles south of Hobetown, had stirred itself into a stew of small homes and trailer parks for whites, blacks, Mexicans, and drifters who were looking for cheap rent. Thelma and James Poteat lived in the oldest mobile home park in the area. The Poteat's lot, one of the original ten, was larger than those nearest the road, where the park owner had squeezed three additional trailers into the already crowded space in violation of the county code. No one complained and that's how things were done in Back Creek. The Poteats had status; not only had they lived there longer than any of their neighbors, but James had always been employed, owned a paid-for late-model car and a pickup.

Thelma, almost six feet tall and strong as most men, looked up from her flower garden when Cameron pulled in and got out of her car.

"Hello. It's been a long time. I'm Cameron Patterson."

"Lord, God," the startled woman replied, brushing the dirt off her shirt. "What are you doing here?"

"I'd like to talk about Nell if you have a minute."

"Is she all right?"

"She's fine. I didn't mean to scare you."

Thelma pointed to the deck attached to the trailer. She didn't want to be rude, so she offered her a chair. She never expected to see this woman again, not after she'd brought Callie, seven months pregnant to Cameron's house twenty years ago. The doctor had arranged with the Pattersons to adopt the baby when it was born. Thelma thought that was the end of it.

"Nice flowers," Cameron said. "You have a pretty place here."

"You like flowers, too." Thelma brushed a pile of papers off the chair before sitting down. "I've drove by your place several times and admired them."

"Thank you." Cameron pulled her chair around to face Thelma. "I started to call but decided just to drive out. Hope you don't mind."

Thelma didn't answer. Of course she minded. What would you expect? She avoided Cameron's eyes and looked at her flowers. Everyone said Thelma had the nicest yard they'd ever seen. No one could grow coleus like that. Each year, before frost, she pinched the tops off and placed them in the window in a fruit jar of water. Early spring she'd have them back out

Cameron Patterson's coleus didn't look nearly as nice as hers, and she felt like telling her that.

"All of a sudden, Nell wants to know about her mother. I don't know what to do about it."

"You been good to her?" Thelma asked.

"As good as I know how to be. She's resented me ever since my husband died. They were close. She thinks she got cheated when it comes to a parent."

Thelma snorted and looked away. "That sounds like her mother."

"Do you think Callie might want to meet her? I know I signed an agreement never to identify her, but I wondered if she's changed her mind. So much time's gone by."

"Callie lives in Florida. She has two more children and a husband that don't know nothin' about Nell. My guess is that's the way she wants it to stay."

Back then Callie had filed for a divorce from her husband, a Marine serving overseas. She'd found another marine, a pilot stationed at a nearby base who got her pregnant. She told the doctor that her pilot wanted to marry her and take her up north where his rich family lived, but he felt it would be better if they put the baby up for adoption. Thelma thought the whole thing sounded fishy, but what could she do? She and James couldn't take care of a baby, and the Pattersons were good people. They could give the baby everything it wanted. They agreed that Callie could stay with them until the baby was born. Callie was impatient; all she wanted was to get the whole thing over with so she could run off with her pilot.

They expected Callie's husband home any day, and she wouldn't leave the Patterson house, afraid she'd run into him on the street. He didn't know about the baby, and Callie and Thelma wanted it to stay that way.

"I'd never violate the privacy agreement," Cameron said. "I'd rather not tell Nell about it, but I'm eventually going to have to tell her something."

"Tell her to thank you for raising her and giving her a good home. Tell her that her mother's husband comes home drunk at least once a month and slaps her around, but she won't leave him 'cause she's too lazy to go to work."

"I'm sorry to hear that. She never heard from Nell's father again?"

Thelma snorted. "What do you think? Before Callie left the hospital, he got called away on a secret mission. Secret mission, all right. You remember that."

"I do remember, but we never knew what happened."

"We raised her first two children after she went off with the fellow she's married to now. They turned out pretty good. She had two more boys after that. One's in jail and the other's about to be."

"Do you think there's any point in mentioning this to Callie?"

"I'll mention it. It's up to her." Thelma took a pack of chewing gum from her pocket and offered Cameron a piece. "Always hoped Nell would amount to something. No one else in this family's had the opportunity she has."

"I'll respect whatever Callie decides. Here's my phone number." Cameron handed Thelma a card. "Call me anytime."

Thelma put the card in her pocket without looking at it, and stood up. "I'll speak to Callie."

CALLIE

Callie couldn't remember the last time her mother had called. "What's the matter?" she asked, certain this had to be more bad news.

"Cameron Patterson come by this morning. Said Nell was wantin' to meet her mother. I told her I didn't think that would work, but I'd let you decide for yourself."

Callie let out a long stream of breath, deflating her bony chest. "Why she want to meet me now?"

"I don't know nothin' about it. She just said Nell's been unhappy since her daddy died."

"All I need is one more problem. You tell that woman that me and her signed a piece of paper, and I expect her to keep her word."

"Told her as much. Don't know what's got into that girl. You'd think she'd appreciate livin' in a big house with nothin' to worry about. I seen her a few times. Be pretty if she tried."

Callie reached for a cigarette and slumped down in the chair. "Some people don't know how good they got it. Wish I'd had the opportunity she did."

She didn't have to tell her mother what a

disgusting life she had—the heat, her husband, her thieving children. They'd drained her of every last penny she had trying to keep them out of jail, and it hadn't done any good. "Wish I had a big house and plenty of money instead of this trash trailer in the hottest hellhole on earth."

"Told Cameron I'd let you know and you decide."

The call irritated Callie. She didn't like stressing her brain with thoughts about the past. She wished she'd never have to think about it again—all those hopes that ended in the trash pile, a lifetime of broken promises and hateful men. If she'd had half the chance Nell had, she'd have been somebody. A few years ago, when she was staying with her folks after she and Joe had a fight, she'd seen Sy Patterson at the checkout counter in the grocery store. Beside him, a teenage girl was pulling on his arm and whining for him to buy her something she was holding. He must have given in because she started laughing and ran out of the store. That's Nell, she realized, grown up and acting like a brat. She'd felt like running out there and slapping her. Who did that girl think she was? Seeing Nell had got under her skin so bad. It had pissed her off the rest of the day and she'd kept thinking about how unfair life was.

She grabbed a Coke from the refrigerator

and slouched back against the kitchen counter. She looked at the Coke can. At least it wasn't alcohol. Joe told her if he came home one more time and found her drunk, he'd kick her out for good. After the last fight, when he'd nearly broken her arm, she believed him.

All these years she'd been jealous of a daughter she'd never known, imagining her living with rich people who gave her anything she'd asked for. She remembered the Pattersons as uppity people who tried to make her think they didn't look down their noses at her. They'd treated her all right, but she never felt comfortable around them. Always thought they should have given her more money. She knew about girls who'd been paid thousands of dollars to have a baby for a couple.

Then an idea occurred to her like a divine revelation. If Nell had all that money and was unhappy and wanted to meet her real mother, maybe she'd be willing to share some of it. Blood's thicker than water.

That idea stayed with her all afternoon. Why shouldn't they meet? Probably when Nell realized what a terrible life her real mother had, she'd want to help her out. She could move out of this goddamn trailer and live somewhere decent for a change.

At four o'clock she decided it wouldn't hurt to have one beer. At five o'clock, and two beers later, she called her mother. "Tell Cameron I've decided I'll meet Nell if that's what she wants, but she needs to pay for it."

"How much you going to need?"

"Much as I can get."

Thelma didn't respond. She held the phone to her ear until Callie spoke.

"Okay. Tell her to send you $500. You can give it to me when I get up there." If she needed more she'd get it out of Nell.

*

When Joe came in from work, Callie told him her mother was sick and she needed to drive up to Hobetown to help out. She wanted to leave tomorrow morning. Joe was more concerned about his Crown Victoria than Callie's uncharacteristic concern for her mother. He didn't like Callie driving his car, and he'd made her swear she wouldn't if she'd been drinking.

Callie wasn't worried about Joe finding out she'd lied about her mother's health. He'd never call up there long distance. He was too cheap and didn't care for Callie's parents. He didn't like the way they stuck it to him about how good Callie's two children from a previous marriage had done, the ones Thelma and James raised.

The more she thought about going up there, the more she liked the idea.

She didn't have a credit card. Joe'd probably give her fifty dollars and tell her not to spend it all in one place. He'd expect her parents to give her whatever she'd need once she got there. That's Joe. If he ever did anything for you he'd expect twice as much in return.

She wanted to buy something to wear, get her hair fixed. She looked at her fingernails, bitten to the quick. She needed acrylics. When she got to Hobetown she'd do something about that. Everything was cheaper up there. Who knows, maybe she wouldn't come back. Why should she? She had a rich daughter up there. Wasn't anything in northern Florida with her name on it.

Her reflection in the bathroom mirror made her angry. Forty-five, but she looked like an old woman. Her thin, stringy hair almost disappeared against her pale skin. The lady at the cosmetic counter at Penney's told her smoking and drinking were worse on a woman's face than age. Examining herself in the mirror, she had to agree. Her lips had shriveled into a highway of creases. She hated the way lipstick snaked up those lines. The heat made it worse. She needed to get those injections that puff up your mouth—needed it around the eyes, too. Except for a flat chest, she still had a good figure—good legs and a hard ass. There wasn't anything the matter with her that money couldn't fix.

After dinner, Joe took the paper and a cigar out to the redwood deck. Callie joined him when she finished the dishes. She unfolded an aluminum chair, then threw it on the floor and kicked it off the deck. "Goddamn birds. Why don't they shit on someone else's porch?"

"They probably do, but other people wash it off."

Callie glared at him and almost took the bait. If she hadn't been leaving the next day she'd have gotten into a fight right there. She looked up at the neighbor's trailer. That nosey bitch was watching. Felt like shooting her the bird. She'd be glad to get away from her too.

Joe waited for the response and when it didn't come, he stood up, stretched his arms and walked down the steps. "Think I'll go to the store and get a beer."

Callie said, "I need some money."

Joe walked a few steps and turned around. "If you're not back by Sunday, I'm coming to get my car."

Tuesday, September 17

BIG MIKE

This was only the second time Mike had been in an airplane, and he tried not to show how nervous it made him.

"Buckle your seatbelt," Michael said.

They planned to fly from Boston to Atlanta and pick up a car. Big Mike figured it would take three hours to drive to Newman's Ridge in Hancock County, Tennessee, a sparsely populated, rugged terrain. He brought along maps and a shopping bag of books and articles about the Melungeons. He handed one to Michael. "Your ma's not happy about us going on this trip. She's been moping around every day since I told her."

"What's she think we're going to do?" Michael didn't want to sound irritated, but he couldn't help being annoyed.

"She's afraid something's gonna happen to you," Big Mike replied.

"If she had her way, I'd never leave home."

"She lives her life differently than most. Just the way she is," Mike said.

"Does she really believe all that stuff about past lives? Was she always like that?"

"Yeah. Had me interested in it for a while. Used to go to the center with her when someone important came to town. Met this fellow at one of the meetings, cantankerous old cuss. He kept interrupting the speaker who was trying to talk about reincarnation. He disagreed with the speaker and said it wasn't reincarnation that made us remember past lives. Said it was genes. All that information is in our genes and gets passed on. Got me to thinking."

"Come on, Big Mike. You don't really believe that genes carry memories from one lifetime to the next."

"Of course they do. That's what genes are. Memories. You don't think they remember where they come from?"

Michael narrowed his eyes and cast Big Mike a sideways glance.

"Don't give me that sour look," Big Mike scolded. "The gene that's got you worried come from someone who had FMF, didn't it? Must have been a Middle Eastern person. And he passed it on, and the next guy passed it on, and so on until it come down to you. It didn't come through the air."

"It didn't come with a pedigree."

"How do you know?"

Michael shook his head.

Big Mike pressed his point. "If a gene can remember one thing, like a disease, then why can't it remember another?"

Michael slapped his grandfather on the knee and squeezed it. "No wonder mom's so weird."

"Your ma's different. I'll give you that."

His daughter wasn't just different. He'd be hard pressed to describe her. She could be downright scary at times. She'd moved home before Michael was born—heartbroken, he figured—but never talked about what had happened. All that changed when Michael came along. He was the only thing that mattered in her life. She said he was a gift and their lives had been foretold. She never made a decision until she had their charts read by those metaphysical folks downtown. She worked there two days a week so she could get free readings. Some of that stuff was okay, but she carried it too far.

An hour into the flight Big Mike looked out the window at the mountains below. "Newman's Ridge is down there somewhere. Never thought I'd see it."

"Growing up in West Virginia, you weren't that far away. Didn't your mother ever go back to the Ridge?"

"You don't understand how it was back then. Folks were born and died in coal towns and some of them never left. The other side of the mountain might as well have been the other side of the ocean."

"You got out."

"Luck, son, pure luck."

Michael waited for him to continue, but Big Mike turned his gaze back to the window.

Flying over the green mountains brought back memories; his father's funeral with a house full of weeping women and men sneaking around drinking liquor out of a fruit jar. He thought about his mother, a tiny woman who rarely smiled. "Trust in the Lord," she'd say when things were bad. "He'll never put more on you than you can bear." He remembered the bone-chilling cold and Sunday morning sermons promising a better life for those who loved Jesus. He would sit patiently, listening, and wondering why they'd have to wait so long. He'd been the oldest of six. His father had died in a mining accident when Mike was in the ninth grade, and he had to leave school and go to work in the mine to help his mother support the family. He might have remained there, dreaming of opportunities beyond his reach, if he hadn't saved the life of a young engineer.

It happened one morning as the sun rose above the mountain cutting through the mist. The year was 1941, and the country was preparing for war. Miners were needed to supply the demand for coal, even those like Mike who'd been born with a twisted leg. He limped up the hill to the mine, swinging his lunch box, thinking about the library book he'd stayed up too late reading, and took his place in the car that would take the miners one mile into the center of the mountain. Eight hours later, when his shift was over, he'd return to daylight.

That morning a young engineer joined them. They rode to the worksite, and the miners began picking a trench along the base of the coalface lining the walls of the shaft. Later, explosives set along the trench would ignite and the coal would collapse. Then he and the other miners would load the coal car and send it out. They knew to watch the overhead beams directly above the dynamite. If they heard any cracking they were to run back toward the mouth of the tunnel. You never knew when one of the beams would break loose.

Miners backed up, waiting for the explosion, while the engineer stood in front of them watching the procedure. They had a good firing; the face tumbled down. "Get back!" one of the men yelled. "That beam's shifting." Instead of running, the engineer looked up to see what was happening just as the beam crashed down pinning him to the ground. The miners, not knowing what happened, instinctively ran to safety.

Mike, who'd been watching the engineer, had seen him crumble to the ground and frantically began digging him out.

Stunned by the crash, the engineer's eyes rolled unfocused then stopped on a spot in the roof. "Get out," he whispered.

Mike followed his gaze to the beam directly above him. Coal dust fell like snow as the beam shifted and groaned from the weight pushing it down. "I'll get you out," Mike said. The next handful of coal he dug out was covered in blood. The beam had sliced across the engineer's thigh severing the artery. With each heartbeat blood spurted from the wound. All Mike knew to do was press his fist against the cut as hard as he could and pray.

"I told you to get out," the engineer repeated. "That beam. . . ."

"I ain't going nowhere," Mike said. "They'll be here in a minute."

Fortunately, help did arrive before the beam came down and both men were rescued.

For saving the engineer's life, Mike's picture appeared in the local paper, and in front of three hundred neighbors he received a signed photograph of the owner of the mine and a check for $100, the most money he'd ever seen. The next day he walked three miles to town to the Miner's Bank and Trust Company, and asked to speak to the person in charge of investments.

The employees recognized him from the picture in the paper and invited him into the president's office. He told the banker he needed advice about how to invest one hundred dollars; he wanted to make money. The president asked him how much he expected to make, and Mike said, without hesitation, four hundred dollars.

The president explained that investing involved risk. "Only way you'll make that kind of money is to steal it," he joked. "But wait a minute." He drummed the desk with his fingers. "Might just be another way. New mine's getting ready to open. I own stock in it. I'll sell you some of my stock. Hold it a couple of years and it'll be worth something."

Mike was confused by the banker's generosity—thought he misunderstood what he said. "You don't know nothin' about me. Why would you do that?"

The banker looked at the tough-minded young man who sat straight in his chair, unflinchingly confident and honest, with a look that dared any man to lie. "I know a whole lot about you. That fellow you kept from bleeding to death was my son."

Big Mike swore that fate took him by the hand that day and walked him those three miles. As it turned out, the banker was right. Four years later, when Mike was nineteen, he sold his stock for $900. With that money he bought tickets on a Greyhound bus for his entire family and moved them to Boston to join his mother's sister. She needed help with their grocery store. Her husband had been drafted during the war but didn't return. Mike eventually bought her out. Over the next five years he doubled the size of the store and bragged that he married the prettiest girl in the neighborhood. Together they ran the store. He sold it and retired when she died. "It's nothing without her," he said.

CAMERON

Cameron opened the gallery Tuesday morning and turned on the radio to catch the ten o'clock weather report. Hurricane Hilda was now a hundred miles south of Cuba and had strengthened overnight to a category three. It could still slam into the Gulf of Mexico, but that wasn't likely. Everything depended on a cold front spreading its way across the Ohio River Valley. If the front advanced as predicted, it would push the monster storm out to sea. Regardless of which path it took, the weather off the Carolina coast shouldn't affect the opening Friday night.

Although small, Selig's collection was the most prestigious show the gallery had exhibited. Publicity had reached collectors as far away as San Francisco. Calls and emails poured in requesting information.

Sy would have been so proud. He'd dreamed of owning a gallery, a venue for the best Southern artists to display their work, including his own watercolors. Looking at him, one would never guess that the quiet, rugged man who hiked through acres of timberland every day was an accomplished painter. They'd spent many Sunday afternoons wandering through abandoned stores and warehouses, imagining how their gallery would look someday.

After Sy's death, Lynne kept the conversation going. It wasn't until they drove past the old Markham home with a "For Rent" sign posted in the window that Cameron got excited. Expansive rooms, ten-foot ceilings and all the light she could ask for. The perfect place. Lynne persuaded other artists to sign on, and it was Lynne who got her hands on a list of collectors who liked nothing better than to drive to a charming little town on the coast and see a first rate show. It wasn't long before artists knocked on Cameron's door. With the help of a smart PR firm in Atlanta, she was established. The gallery was small, requiring only Cameron and one assistant to run it. She'd hoped that Nell would be interested, but so far that wasn't happening.

As excited as she was about the new show, Cameron hated to see Lynne's come down. Her work had always been good, but something transformational had happened. She felt Lynne had found a new source for inspiration. The realism that distinguished her work was still there, hidden beneath an abstraction that tantalized the viewers, luring them to examine the painting for its secrets, but this new work was bolder, more confident.

"You've reached a new level," Cameron had said to Lynne, as they waited for the guests to arrive on her opening night.

Lynne had walked from one canvas to the next, studying each as if seeing it for the first time. "I've been painting twenty years. I feel I'm looking at someone else's work." She turned to Cameron and winked. "Damn good work."

*

Thelma had left a phone message—Callie was coming, call her. A pain shot up the back of Cameron's neck. She kneaded the spot, knowing it wouldn't go away until she returned the call. She'd enjoyed a false sense of relief after she'd talked to Thelma, assuming Callie would reject the reunion. She hadn't thought through what would happen if Callie wanted to meet the child she'd abandoned for the pilot who'd abandoned her.

Thelma was waiting for Cameron's call. "Callie says she wants to meet Nell."

"When is she coming?"

"Tomorrow."

Cameron felt a pounding in her head.

"I hate to bother you about this, but Callie's going to need money when she gets up here." Cameron heard embarrassment in Thelma's voice. She wasn't the kind of woman who enjoyed taking money from the person who'd raised her granddaughter.

"I'll put a check in the mail today and you should get it tomorrow."

"That'll be fine. Mighty good of you, You want Callie to come to your place?"

No went off inside her head at the thought of that complaining, angry young woman coming to her house. "I'll talk to Nell and call you in the morning. Better let her decide where to meet."

*

Cameron was still at her desk, wondering what to do about Callie, when the phone rang, startling her.

"I hope it's not too late to accept your invitation to the opening," Dr. Rao said.

"Not at all. I'm happy you can come." Cameron tried to sound matter-of-fact, the way she'd talk to any guest. He hadn't been on her guest list, and this show of Indian art was the perfect excuse to add him.

"Also, I wonder if you could come a few minutes early for your appointment. I'd like to talk to you about a referral."

"Referral?"

"Would that be convenient?"

"Actually, Dr. Rao, I should probably cancel today's appointment. I've just found out that Nell's mother is coming tomorrow, and I've got to take down this show, and…." She paused and laughed. "I'm over my head."

"Sounds like you need to come. Would it

help if we rescheduled for later this evening? I could see you at seven."

Cameron pictured him at his polished desk wearing a long-sleeved shirt, cuff links and conservative tie, the bodhisattva looking over his shoulder. "You're right. I do need to come. Seven is fine."

She hung up the phone with "referral" ringing in her ear. What was he talking about? She hadn't referred anyone to him.

The back door opened and Lynne walked in, head down, dragging slow, deliberate steps.

"What's wrong?" Cameron asked.

Lynne slumped into a chair. "You'll gloat if I tell you."

"Buddy?"

"He swears there's nothing to it, but he's hired that little whore Sarah as night clerk."

"Sarah's not a whore."

"You're right. She doesn't charge. Gives it away."

"You've seen them together?"

"I've seen the way they look at each other. And Buddy's staying late at night to check on the accounts. Sure. The accounts between her legs."

"Kick him out. He shouldn't be staying with you anyway."

Lynne threw her head back and stared at the ceiling before she spoke. "Has it ever occurred to you how much we are alike in our choice of men?"

"You've got to be kidding."

"I'm dead serious. You give me hell because I'm attracted to young guys, too young. I admit it. But whom are you attracted to? Not one of the respectables you have everything in common with. Several men have had the hots for you, but no. You wait till someone comes along like Mark, a wolf in sheep's clothing. And when that doesn't work out, guess what? You find an Indian! Who's next, Jesse Jackson?"

"You're crazy."

"Don't tell me you're not attracted to your shrink. Your eyes light up every time you mention his name."

"I see him because I need professional help."

"Bullshit. You see him because you want to get him in bed. You're just like me, Cameron. It's the otherness that attracts us. Strange fruit. Admit it."

*

Cameron realized Dr. Rao had asked her a direct question and was waiting for a response. "I'm sorry. Would you say that again?"

"Why have these two life-altering events collided?" he repeated. "You could have stalled the meeting between Nell and her mother. Why didn't you?"

"Didn't think that Callie would really come and I could tell Nell that she'd have to be content with me. Before I could get that out of the way, Michael appeared."

He lowered his voice. "I get the feeling your mind is somewhere else. What's going on?"

Cameron crumpled in her chair and rubbed the muscle at the back of her neck that was shooting pains down her shoulder. She sighed and looked away, not wanting to meet his eyes. "I was attacked and nearly raped seven years ago by an acquaintance who is now the chief of police. Sy had only been dead three months." Cameron paused.

Dr. Rao raised his eyebrows, leaned forward and crossed his hands on the desk. "I see," he said, and waited.

"I know what you're thinking. Why didn't I tell you this before?"

He shook his head and smiled. "I'm thinking we're finally getting some place."

"It's been on my mind constantly since my friend and I talked about it the other night. If the man I was in love with could rape my daughter, what does that say about me? What kind of men do I attract?"

"Nell wasn't raped. She threw him out."

Cameron interrupted. "His intent was to rape her."

"Until the three of us sit down and talk, we don't know anyone's intent."

Cameron started to protest.

"As painful as this is for you, I feel encouraged. You're ready for serious work. You do know that these two incidents are not related except in your mind. Both of these men sound like scoundrels. Why is it so hard for you to believe that you fell in love with a scoundrel? Women do it all the time." He laughed softly. "That's what keeps me in business."

At the end of the hour Cameron rose to leave, buoyed with relief. Dr. Rao had drawn from her the admission that her need to develop a relationship with Michael wasn't healthy and destined to bring disappointment. No more family research, he chided, no more excuses to establish a bond with Michael. Transference, he called it. Her daughter needed her full attention.

As he spoke Cameron thought about what Lynne had said. The "otherness" attracted him to her. What would it be like, the two of them?

NELL

"I'm home," Nell called out and flopped on the sofa.

Cameron walked into the living room, wiping her hands on a dishtowel. "Where have you been?"

"Where could I go without any money? Beth's place."

Nell expected the usual remarks about Beth not being the kind of person she should be hanging out with. Instead, Cameron settled in an armchair and reached for her hand. "We need to talk, about your mother."

Nell bristled. "What's going on?"

"She's coming to meet you."

"When?"

"Tomorrow."

Nell closed her eyes.

"This isn't easy for either of us," Cameron said. "But you need to know things."

Cameron explained how the young woman named Callie, Nell's biological mother, had come into their lives. She told her about the two children Callie already had who lived with their grandparents at Back Creek, about the father of

Callie's baby who'd come to the house twice, concerned about her welfare. He'd insisted on paying all medical expenses. Nell interrupted and wanted to know more about him, but Cameron only knew that his name was Robert Harrison, and he was from Massachusetts. She remembered him as well-spoken, tall, blond, and very good looking.

"Why didn't you tell me this before?"

"It's what Callie wanted. She thought it would be best for you."

"Bullshit. I've been living this close to my grandparents and never knew it. Why is that better for me?"

"It just seemed the best thing at the time." Cameron reached in her pocket and pulled out a hundred dollar bill. "Buy yourself something nice to wear."

Nell took the money, walked to her bedroom and closed the door.

Wednesday, September 18

NELL

The next morning Nell still lay across her bed fully clothed, thinking about Callie, a name she'd never heard before, and a tall handsome man named Robert. It sounded to her like trailer park trash meets fast-talking Marine pilot and gets dumped when he finds out she's pregnant. She'd never thought much about her biological parents, always assumed they were a local young couple, unmarried and unable to raise a child, who did everyone a favor by giving her up for adoption. But Callie already had two children. One more wouldn't have killed her. And if Robert was such a standup guy, why didn't he want to keep his own daughter?

She'd only said she wanted to meet her real mother to get a reaction. She'd never intended for it to get this far. If Cameron hadn't been so eager to get rid of her, none of this would have happened. She couldn't back out now. Callie was on her way. She looked at the money. "Buy your self something nice to wear." Why should she look nice for the woman who didn't want her?

When she heard Cameron's alarm clock go off she got up, grabbed her pocketbook and walked outside to her car. She'd changed her mind a dozen times during the night about what she wanted to do. She'd drive to Back Creek and meet her grandmother. Cameron said she was a kind, loving woman who wanted the best for the granddaughter she'd never known. Maybe her real mother had been sorry all these years and wanted to make it up to her. Her grandmother would know, but first she needed to stop at the Quikie Mart to fill the gas tank and get something to eat.

A group of men stood outside the cinder-block building, hands in their pockets, eyes riveted on every car that pulled up, while they waited for one to come along and offer them a day job. She entered the building and pushed her way through the line of customers waiting to pay for coffee, packaged foods and cigarettes. From the row of plastic-wrapped food she chose a cinnamon bun that hit her stomach like poison. She barely made it to the restroom to throw up. Her head spun, and she sat on the toilet lid, fighting back waves of nausea.

"What are you doing in there, Nell?" the store clerk demanded, knocking on the door.

"I'll be out in a minute."

"Someone else needs to get in."

"Tell them to use the men's."

She pulled herself up, walked to the sink and splashed her face with cold water. The reflection in the mirror startled her. Mascara streaked down her cheeks, and her hair stood on end, greasy and wild. If she was going to Back Creek to meet her grandmother, she couldn't go looking like this. She grabbed a handful of paper towels and soap, and began to scrub.

She wanted her grandmother to like her. She didn't remember much about Cameron's mother, the woman she'd been named after. She'd died when Nell was six years old. Grandpa Will died later the same year And then her father. It seemed like people were always dying in her adopted family. Let my grandmother like me, she said, under her breath. Let her be someone who wants me.

Feeling self-conscious without her mask of makeup, she walked out of the restroom, her hair washed clean of the flamingo tint and combed flat against her head. She picked up a new tee shirt with "…no country like Low country…" stenciled across the back and tossed it on the counter.

"That took you long enough. You get thrown out?" Marvin, the gangly clerk with a missing front tooth asked. "Can't dress at home?"

"Mind your own business." She put the hundred-dollar bill on the counter. "Got sick eating that crap you sell for food."

His eyes widened at the sight of the bill.

"Nobody told you to eat it."

*

Nell knew exactly where to find the Ponderosa Trailer Park. She'd been there a few times with friends, late at night, looking for pot. She stopped at the row of mailboxes and spotted Poteat #8, then turned into the circular driveway and followed the numbers stuck in the ground in front of each trailer. The nerve it took to walk to the door almost made her throw up again. She stood frozen before she raised her hand and knocked. A tall woman with sad looking eyes opened the door. She wore Bermuda shorts and a flowered blouse.

"Thelma Poteat?" Nell asked. "I'm...."

"I know who you are. Come in." The invitation felt like a command, and Nell stepped inside the trailer.

"Maybe I shouldn't have come, but my mother said—I mean Cameron said that my real mother is coming today."

Thelma nodded. "Yes. Callie's coming this afternoon."

Nell looked around the spotlessly clean trailer. Dark plaid upholstered sofa and chairs with bulky wooden arms, lacy bits of cloths spread over the back cushions. A braided rug of faded colors covered the floor. Artificial flowers spilled out of a vase on the coffee table and plastic vines trailed from a swinging iron planter on the wall. It reminded Nell of her old playhouse and she broke into a wide grin.

"I really like your place," she said, her eyes bright with excitement.

Thelma pointed to the recliner. "Have a seat."

Nell sat down. She couldn't tell if Thelma was upset to see her. She didn't want her to be. "Pretty." She fingered the circular lace behind her head.

"Doilies. Made them myself," Thelma said.

Nell looked surprised.

"From balls of string. Made the rug, too."

"You didn't!"

"Used old clothes people cast off."

"I can't believe it." Nell wouldn't have been more impressed if Thelma had said she'd erected the Eiffel Tower. "Wish I could make something like that."

Thelma smiled, the tension released from her face. "Nothing to it child. Just takes patience. Something your ma, Callie, don't have." She reached under the sofa and pulled out a bag. "I'm working on another rug right now. You just take this cloth and cut it into strips, sew 'em together, then braid it just like this." She held up a coil of twisted fabric. "I'm making this one for the church raffle. Do it every year."

"I'll help," Nell said, and sat up on the edge of the recliner. "If you'll let me."

Thelma put the rug down and walked into the kitchen. "I was just fixing to make a cup of tea when you drove up. Want one?"

"Sure."

"Are you hungry?"

"Kinda. I left home without breakfast."

Thelma put two slices of bread in the toaster and reached in the refrigerator for butter and jam. She put them on the dinette table. "This'll keep you till lunchtime."

When Nell finished her tea and toast, she sat back and looked around at the pictures on the wall. She could imagine what Lynne and Cameron would say about them, and she felt a flush of anger.

Thelma put her cup of tea on the table and sat down across from Nell. "I don't know how to say this without sounding mean-spirited, but don't get your hopes too high about your real mother. She's had a hard life. Turned her bitter. You have a brother and sister in Savannah that have done real good, and they'd like to know you. You'd like 'em. You have two younger brothers in jail. They're not bad. Just took up with the wrong crowd. Callie thinks it's all their fault. If I was you, I wouldn't say anything to her about them."

Nell nodded her head. "I'd like to know more about my father."

"You'll have to ask Callie about that."

Nell rose from the chair and carried her dish

to the sink. "Thanks so much. That's just what I needed. Think I'll go home and change. I'll come back this evening if that's all right?"

"Come for dinner. Spend the night if you like. We have an extra bedroom."

Nell considered that possibility before she answered. "I'd like that. Do you think it would be all right with Callie?"

"Why not? She's coming to meet you. Give ya'll a chance to get to know one another."

"Let's see how it goes." Nell walked to the door, then came back and gave Thelma a hug. "I don't care what happens. I have you."

"And your grandpa." Thelma patted her shoulder. "Just wait till he meets you."

*

On the drive back to Hobetown, Nell wondered if going back was the right thing to do. It hadn't occurred to her that she might spend the night with her grandparents. But why not? Her grandmother thought it was a good idea, but it frightened her. What about her grandfather? Would he like her? And the mother who gave her away? Still, she wanted to be with them. It felt good being wanted.

She needed to fix herself up before she went back. She looked a mess. First, she'd get some sleep. She was exhausted.

The house was empty. Cameron had left a

message to call her at the gallery. Nell couldn't bring herself to talk to her now. Everything was too complicated.

MICHAEL

By the time Michael and Big Mike picked up the rental car, it was late evening, so they spent the night outside the city and started out early the next morning. Several times Michael pulled off the road to sit and stare across the mountains. The higher ridges rising above the blue mists of the valleys were singed with yellow, the first sign of autumnal changes soon to come. He felt the same sense of awe that he experienced when he stood on the shore and looked out at the endless ocean.

Big Mike had made reservations at the Holiday Inn in Vardy, Tennessee, where they would meet Mahala Collins Weaver, their contact from The Vardy Historical Association. She would be their guide for the day and take them to Newman's Ridge. Ms. Weaver, the author of most of the pamphlets and books Big Mike had ordered from the Melungeon Association, was the expert. The three-hour drive stretched to four making them thirty minutes late for their appointment.

"Haley's been waiting for you," the desk clerk at the motel told Big Mike. "Over yonder in the coffee shop."

Mahala Collins Weaver, wearing blue jeans

and a red flannel shirt, walked into the lobby carrying a cup of coffee, and flashed a confident smile of welcome. Big Mike saw a petite, young woman with an honest, pretty face that told him right away he'd like her. He stepped forward and introduced himself. Michael saw a wispy figure barely larger than a child, dressed in hiking clothes and laced-up boots that clanked on the tile floor. Her round, wide-set dark eyes were points of light that shown, friendly and expectant. He also saw clear, olive skin and silky brown hair that hung to her waist, sun-streaked with gold. She wore no make-up or jewelry except a tiny emerald in the side of her nose. He'd never seen a woman like her.

"I'm Haley," she greeted and held out her hand, ready to take charge. "Y'all want to check into your room before we take off?" She looked at her watch.

"We can do that when we come back," Big Mike replied. "No need to keep you waiting any longer."

They followed her across the parking lot to an ancient pickup. "If you don't mind ridin' in this old truck, I'll drive." She smiled at Big Mike. "The roads are too rough for your car."

"Fine with me." Big Mike opened her door. "Can't think of anything I'd rather do than ride around with a pretty lady."

Michael, following behind, hadn't spoken a word. He couldn't take his eyes off the tiny creature. Haley didn't seem to notice. Big Mike gave him a nudge.

When they were seated in the cab she reached across Michael, squeezed in the middle and pulled a pint of whiskey from the glove compartment. Removing the cap, she poured a splash into her coffee. "Helps my nerves." She grinned at them. "First time I've ever taken folks out on a tour." She returned the bottle, then laughed a soft musical sound that reminded Michael of his mother when she was happy. "Truth is there's not much to tour, but I'll stay with y'all as long as you need me."

Haley took a sip and offered it to Michael. "Want some? It'll take the chill out of your bones. We've had a hard spell of cool weather for this time of year."

Michael shook his head. He stared at Haley so intently that Big Mike poked him in the ribs.

"My old bones could use warming up." Big Mike took a hot gulp.

Haley grabbed the steering wheel with both hands and ground the starter till the engine fired. She smiled at Big Mike, and stole a quick glance at Michael, before shoving the floor-stick in high gear and heading off across the parking lot.

"That old church over there has been turned into a museum." She pointed to a newly painted building with a wooden cross on the top. "There's a lot of good material inside. And back there, the great big building that's falling down, that's what's left of the Vardy School. Presbyterian missionaries built it in 1897 when they came here to educate all the children in the valley. Melungeons were banned from white schools."

"It's in terrible shape," Big Mike remarked.

"They're gonna tear it down."

Michael looked out the window at the collapsing three-storied frame building.

"First solar heat in these parts," Haley said. "Ninety-six windows kept it warm in the winter. Had a cafeteria, infirmary, museum, and workshop available to everyone in the community. Oh, and indoor privies, another first."

Michael spoke for the first time. "Seems a shame not to restore it."

"More than a shame," Haley said, her voice falling away in sadness. "But it would cost too much, and no one's interested in an old building in the middle of nowhere."

*

Late afternoon they left the ridge where nothing remained of the cabins but scattered logs and pieces of tin roofing and returned to Vardy Church. Michael didn't think there was a foot of ground on Newman's Ridge that Haley hadn't walked them over. If his legs ached, he couldn't imagine how his grandfather felt.

Haley pointed to a long log cabin across the road, book-ended by stone fireplaces, sitting in an open field.

"That's my great, great grandma's house, Mahala Collins Mullins. I'm named after her." Haley looked wistfully at the two-story house with its wraparound porch. "Pretty, isn't it? Used to be up on the ridge, but the historical society decided to move it down here. I don't reckon I have much in common with her." She glanced at Michael, "Except the love of this country. She birthed twenty-one children right there." Haley's eyes slowly moved over the house, a smile lighting her soft eyes.

"She made the best whiskey on the ridge—supported her family that way. The revenuers never could shut her down."

"I'll bite. How come, Haley?" Mike asked.

"Cause she weighed over five hundred pounds. The government men would come blasting up the hill and tell her she was under arrest and they were going to take her to jail, and she'd say, 'Fine, take me.' But couldn't none of them lift her, and if they did get her on her feet, they couldn't get her out the door 'cause it wasn't wide enough."

Big Mike threw his head back and laughed.

"It's the truth. When she died they had to take the chimney down to get her out of the house so they could bury her."

"Haley, you beat all I've ever heard. You know that's not true."

"True as every word in the gospel. Her granddaddy was old Vardy Collins. Town's named after him. He was the first Melungeon on the ridge. Told everyone he was Portyghee."

Big Mike headed to a bench. Haley followed and squatted on the ground beside him, her long hair falling around her like a velvet cloak.

"You've paid for the first class tour, so I'm bound to give you my spiel about Melungeon history," she said, settling on the ground, pulling her legs under her. "There's several legends about them. One is that Mediterranean pirates sailed up the Cape Fear River to escape capture, abandoned ship and fled to the mountains. Another is that Sir Frances Drake captured a Portuguese ship in the Caribbean. The crew was Middle Eastern sailors and Drake brought them to Jamestown and left them there. Eventually they went west and intermarried with the Indians, which explains many of our characteristics."

"What characteristics?" Michael asked.

"Skin tone like Mediterraneans and speech patterns. Genetic diseases."

Big Mike kicked the dirt with the toe of his shoe. "That's kind of why we came down here. We're curious about those diseases."

"People who claim Melungeon ancestry have figured out there's an uncommon number of them who get diseases that only Middle Eastern people get. This seemed odd being as they weren't Middle Eastern, or didn't think they were. A group of them got together and did some research."

"I personally think we're from survivors of

an earlier group of Portuguese. They'd settled around Charleston in the sixteenth century and their leader, a fella named Prado, sent them out to establish settlements along a trail from Georgia up through North Carolina. After Portugal pulled out, the settlers, men and women, stayed on and took up Indian ways. They kept moving further west, away from the whites. My thinking is that's where we came from. No one knows for sure about the name. Could be from the French word, *mélang.* Others say it's *melungo*, which is Portuguese for shipmate. Then there's the notion that it's from the Arabic *melun jinn,* which means cursed soul. Who knows? Whatever its source, they were treated like people of color."

"Understand they have a big gathering of Melungeon descendants up here once a year," Big Mike said.

"You ought to come," Haley replied. "Won't be long before no one will remember what a Melungeon was. If it weren't for the diseases no one would ever have heard about these people. So much intermarriage and indifference makes folks forget or some not want to remember. I don't want their history to disappear. Hasn't been so long ago that being a Melungeon was a shameful thing. That's mostly changed. Why are ya'll interested? Got family from up around here?"

"My mother was from Newman's Ridge," Big Mike replied. "She left here and married my daddy who was a coal miner in West Virginia. We never met her family. She didn't talk about them much, but she use to tell us how beautiful the ridge was, and how much she missed it."

"What was her name?"

"Evaline Collins. Same as your grandma Mahala."

"That doesn't surprise me. Near about everyone in the county was named Collins, or married to a Collins at one time. Guess that makes us kind of cousins."

When they got back to the motel, Big Mike asked Haley if she could take Michael to dinner. He'd heard about a famous barbeque place nearby that he'd wanted to try, but he was tuckered out and hoped she and Michael would go without him. He'd get something in the coffee shop.

"Can we go like this?" Michael asked looking down at his jeans and boots.

"That's the way we go around here." Sensing Michael's uncertainty she added. "I can go home and change if it would make you feel better."

"You look great. I'll just kick the mud off my boots and be ready to go."

Michael waited in the rental car outside the motel while Haley called to check on her three-year-old daughter.

"Everything's okay," she said, and slid in beside him. "Mama said Mindy could spend the night."

"I didn't realize you were married," Michael said.

"Why would I be going off with you if I had a husband?"

Michael felt the color rise up his neck. "Just thought, since you had a little girl…"

"That I was married? You don't have to be married to have children."

He couldn't think of anything to say, so he sat quietly until she spoke again. "Which one of the diseases do you have?"

Michael hadn't told her he had a disease. Big Mike probably had. "FMF. At least, they think I do"

"That's the one you get from both parents, isn't it?"

"Yes." He paused, not wanting to talk about it, but she kept watching and waiting for him to reply. "My parents weren't married and I didn't know my father. Big Mike was the one who found out his mother was a Melungeon. We hoped to get someone down here to research my father's family, Pattersons from North Carolina."

"Melungeon name all right. If your daddy is a descendant, he'll likely be in our database. I can check it out for you."

"I'll be glad to pay you."

Haley dismissed the offer with a toss of her head. "This must be worrisome for you. Right off I knew something was wrong 'cause you've been so quiet." She gave him a little slap on the arm. "I was even wondering if you were all right in the head."

Michael grinned. "I'm beginning to wonder about that myself."

By the time they got to the restaurant Michael was laughing out loud at Haley's stories of mountain people. He couldn't believe anyone could be so smart, even sophisticated, yet so down-to-earth. He'd never heard anyone speak like her.

"My grandfather said we'd meet a little old lady who'd show us around. Imagine how surprised I was to find you."

"Hope you're not too disappointed," Haley said.

He made a sad face. "I'll get over it."

"Come back in a few years and you'll find that old lady."

"Don't you ever plan to leave this place? See what's out there?"

"I'm a mountain girl. Moved away a couple of times, but I came back home. Can't imagine living in a big city like you do. Not that there's anything the matter with it, but I need fresh air that someone, or something, hasn't used first. I love these hills. They're beautiful all year. You should see what the first big snow looks like. Covers the ground like a blanket of goose feathers."

The restaurant looked like a run-down barn to Michael, inside and out. Tables covered with checked oilcloth sported a collection of bottles filled with brown liquid. A trio of musicians belted out Country Western songs at the far end of the restaurant for a group of energetic couples performing synchronized dance steps. Haley picked out a table beside the fireplace and ordered for both of them.

Michael held up one of the bottles.

"Put it on your barbeque." Haley pointed to each bottle as she spoke. "That one's hot. That one's not so hot, and that one's red hot."

She shook a drop from the hottest bottle on her finger and put it in Michael's mouth.

"Good God," he yelled, and grabbed a glass of water.

Haley giggled. "Now you know. Always taste it first."

When the heaping plates of finely cut barbeque, coleslaw and French fries came, Haley took her time explaining the difference between South Carolina and Tennessee barbeque. "Every state swears theirs is the best," she said. "Most places take shortcuts nowadays, but what you're eating here is cooked the old fashioned way. Hickory smoked over a slow fire in a brick oven with red pepper and vinegar. What do you think?"

"Might be better than what I had in South Carolina. I'll have to come back and have some more before I decide. Would that be a good idea?"

"I reckon." A smile played across her face.

*

"Want to come in?" Haley asked when they

drove up to her trailer, hidden in a copse of trees behind Vardy church. "Looks worse out here than inside."

"Sure," he answered, eying an aged silver Airstream propped on cinderblocks. "You got a cold beer?"

The door opened onto a sitting room, kitchen combination. "All I could afford while I was going to school." A hint of shame crept into her voice. "Could have stayed at home but that wasn't fair to Mama. She took care of Mindy during the day. Least I could do was get out of her hair at night."

Michael looked around. There wasn't much furniture: a sofa, two easy chairs and an old wooden trunk that served as a coffee table. Lamps made from mountain pottery sat on rustic end tables, their edges rounded from wear. These were the kind of pieces his mother looked at longingly in antique shops.

"Hand-me-downs from my granny," Haley said.

A painting of the mountains grabbed his attention. He'd wanted something like this when he furnished his apartment, but Steff had talked him into buying a contemporary painting from a local gallery. "That is really nice."

"Bill Dunlap. I was a student of his. Corrected papers a year to get it."

"Any time you want to get rid of it…"

"Going in my new house. I own this land and I hope to build as soon as I start my job.

Bankers won't lend you any money till they know you can pay it back. Guess you know all about that."

"Where will you be working?"

"Starting next semester, I'll be teaching history at the Community College."

"That's great, Haley."

"Well, don't look so surprised. Guess you didn't think…"

Michael took Haley by the shoulders and turned her around. She couldn't weigh a hundred pounds, he thought.

"Stop picking on me." He grinned and looked down into her nearly black eyes. "I'm thinking that you're the most interesting, gorgeous woman I've ever met."

She wriggled out of his grasp and took two beers from the refrigerator.

They clinked bottles and Michael caught the look in her eyes that told him Haley Mullins, miniature spitfire, liked what she saw.

"I'd really like to get to know you," he said. "We're leaving tomorrow, but I can come back."

She shook her head indifferently.

"Would that be all right with you?"

"Why'd you want to mess around with a hillbilly like me, you being a fancy lawyer and all that?"

"Who told you I was a lawyer?"

"Your grandpa."

"You didn't answer my question."

"Reckon it'd be all right if you haven't anything else to do."

Michael sat on the sofa and patted the space beside him.

"Want to watch TV?" she asked.

"No. I'd rather talk to you."

"That's all right, but don't go getting any ideas about spending the night."

At that moment he could think of nothing he'd rather do, but he kissed her on the forehead and settled back on the sofa. "Let's talk."

CAMERON

Cameron and Lynne played doubles tennis every Wednesday morning at the Hobetown Country Club. The unpretentious two-story brick clubhouse sat on the banks of the Greasy River beneath ancient live oaks that spread their scaly branches across the rolling lawn.

Lynne hadn't been a member since her divorce from Hubie Odum six years ago, but she continued her weekly game.

Lynne waited on her steps for Cameron to pick her up. "I understand someone complained about me not being a member," she said, and climbed in the car.

"Who told you that?"

"Hubie. I ran into him at the grocery store. One of the new members said since I didn't pay dues, I shouldn't have privileges. We don't have to play."

"Yes, we do," Cameron insisted. "I need the exercise, and I'm not about to find another partner. To hell with these new people."

After their match Cameron wanted to go to the golf shop for a cup of coffee. Lynne followed, indifferent, until she saw Hubie Odum at the counter buying golf balls. Hubie, the jokester, the guy that got everyone laughing, had put on weight over the past years, but despite graying temples and deep creases slicing each cheek, he still had a boyish look about him.

Lynne grabbed the back of Cameron's shirt. "Let's get out of here."

Cameron ignored her. They ran into Hubie all the time, and Lynne usually paid no attention to him.

Hubie looked up. "Hello, ladies. Have a good game?" He called out to Lynne as she crossed the room to get coffee. "I told the Board not to worry about your membership, honey. I'll take care of your guest fee."

Lynne turned her back to Hubie.

Cameron pulled the yellowed Polaroid from her pocketbook and held it up for Hubie to see. "Look what I found."

Hubie examined the picture. "Goddamn. That's me and Sy. Look at all that hair."

"Who's the woman?"

"Where'd you find it?"

"With Sy's things. Who is she?"

Cameron moved closer, holding the photograph in his face. The tennis pro behind the counter sensed the tension and backed away.

"What the hell are you women up to?" Hubie glanced from Lynne to Cameron. "Why don't you ask Lynne about Sy's girlfriends?" The words shot out of his mouth like a snake striking its prey. He pushed the old photograph away and stalked out.

Lynne put the coffee cup down and hurried out the door to the car. Cameron followed.

"What's wrong with Hubie? Surely he remembers her."

"He's crazy," Lynne replied.

"What did he mean—ask Lynne about Sy's girlfriends?"

"How do I know? He'll say anything to get me upset. Why don't you leave him alone? At least when I'm around." She looked away, angry.

"Because I want him to tell me about that woman. I have a right to know."

Lynne took her time lighting a cigarette before she answered. "No, you don't, Cameron. That ended before you and Sy got serious. Did you tell Sy about the guys you dated at college? I remember one in particular." Lynne rolled her eyes.

"That's different."

"No, it's not. Send the picture back to Michael and forget it."

Cameron hurried home, showered and changed, then drove to the gallery, all the while trying to understand what had happened in the pro shop. What did Hubie mean about Sy's girlfriends? Why was Lynne so angry?

Recently Lynne had been on edge, sardonic. Something was bothering her. She'd sworn she knew nothing about the woman in the picture. Lynne wouldn't lie to her. But what had set Hubie off? Something was going on.

*

Cameron spent the rest of the day going over the invitation list for the opening, making sure she knew the names of the people who'd accepted and where they lived. She kept a card index of everyone on her database, with personal notations such as, "Emily is his second wife, and she hates everything he and his first wife bought from me." She relied on these gossipy quips.

Unless the guests got cold feet at the last minute, they'd have the largest crowd ever. But her excitement about the show had been dampened by the morning's scene in the pro shop. Why had Hubie hurled such a hateful remark at her? "Ask Lynne about Sy's girlfriends," he'd snarled, as if Lynne had been one. As if Sy had girlfriends. Truth was Sy avoided Lynne. He found her belligerent and rude, particularly when she drank too much, which was most of the time back then. That created a problem because Hubie and Sy had always been best friends, and it was natural that the young couples would hang around together. Hubie knew all that, so what would possess him to make such a nasty remark?

A few minutes before closing time, she locked up and walked across the parking lot. A window rolled down in the car parked next to hers, and Hubie Odum stuck out his head.

"Cameron." He flashed a big grin. "Just coming to get you. Let me buy you a drink." He leaned across the front seat and opened the door. "Get in."

Cameron slid in beside him. "What's going on? You haven't bought me a drink in years. Trying to make up to me for acting like a jackass this morning?"

Hubie chuckled. "I was out of line. Shouldn't have said what I did about Lynne, but you girls looked like two penned-up pit bulls when you walked in the shop. Scared the hell out of me."

"I just wanted to know who the woman was in the picture. Lynne had nothing to do with it. What did you mean about Sy's girlfriends?"

"Honey, I was running my mouth. Lynne looked ill as a hornet, and I thought she was going to start something. She still bugs me about money she thinks I owe her. That woman can be downright crazy at times."

Hubie pulled into the empty parking lot beside the cafe. The evening drinkers had not arrived. He removed his tie and threw it in the back seat.

Cameron looked across the pavement toward the river. The parking lot, a shade lighter than the sun-bleached boardwalk, seemed to melt into the murky river. Shimmers of heat rose from the asphalt. She wished she hadn't agreed to join Hubie for a drink. She didn't need an apology, and she didn't need to hear about his miserable life with Lynne.

"What you looking at?" Hubie asked.

"Just thinking how gray everything is this time of year."

He looked up. "Know what you mean. Can't tell where the sky ends and the river begins. Soon as the hurricane passes we'll get some clean air."

Cameron walked toward the door. "Didn't mean to be so glum. I've had a bad week."

"Me too, hon," Hubie said.

Steve was leaning across the bar watching the weather report on TV. The slightest lift of an eyebrow hid any surprise he might have at seeing Cameron and Hubie together. "How ya'll doing," he said.

"Hurricane going to hit us?" Hubie asked.

"Don't know. Sure tearing up those islands. What can I get you folks?"

Hubie pointed toward the river. "Couple of gin and tonics out on the porch."

Cameron followed him out the door. "Hubie, what's going on? You and Maggie having trouble?"

"No, honey, nothing like that. She's the best thing that ever happened to me. Wish I'd met her before I fell in love with Lynne and nearly ruined my life. I hate to say it, but Lynne's about the worst thing that ever happened to me."

Hubie pulled out a chair for Cameron and then sat across from her. "After I left you this morning, I went home and talked to Maggie. Told her what I said to Lynne. She said I needed to talk to you." The vein in Hubie's forehead beat a cadence; the perspiration glistened on his turgid face. "Said I need to get it off my chest. Sy's death was my fault. I could have saved him. I've wanted to tell you—should have—but I just couldn't. Lynne and I fought about it. She felt guilty too, and it got to where we couldn't stand to look at each other."

Steve put two drinks on the table then retreated. Hubie took a long swallow and motioned for Steve to bring another round even though Cameron hadn't touched hers. She raised her hand to object but Hubie interrupted, "Don't worry about it, honey. I'll drink it."

"Saturday night before we went out fishing we were all at the club together. Remember that night?"

She remembered Sy hadn't wanted to go. He hated those once-a-month buffets at the country club—young married couples dressed up, ate, drank,` and danced to the rhythm of a local band. It was a time for the ladies to show off new clothes and catch up on gossip. All the men wanted to talk about was the marlin tournament the next day. For months they'd been getting ready for the annual event. All the top fishermen in the state would be on the water before dawn. She and Sy left the club earlier than the others, but that wasn't unusual.

"What about it?" Cameron asked.

"We were all loaded. God, we used to drink, didn't we?" He took a sip of his gin and tonic and held up the glass. "Knocked these babies down like water. Anyway, I saw Sy on the terrace and started out there to talk to him when Lynne came around the corner. She was high, which didn't excuse her, but she was all over him. Saw the whole thing and I walked out and grabbed her. Sy didn't know I'd been watching, and he wasn't going to say that she practically attacked him. I was so goddamn mad I wanted to kill her."

"Why are you telling me this?"

Perspiration snaked down Hubie's slack jaws and he unfolded his drink napkin and wiped his face. "The next morning while we packed the gear on the boat, Sy came up to me and said he was sorry about what had happened, but there was nothing to it. I knew there wasn't, as far as he was concerned. Sy wasn't going to say my wife was a slut. He said something about we'd all had too much to drink and let's forget it, but no, my pride was hurt, and I wouldn't let it go. After we'd set the lines, one of them fouled. Sy yelled for Pete to trim the motor so he could untangle it. He asked me to hold the other lines, but I told him to fix it himself and went below to make a sandwich. When I came back up there was no one on deck. I thought Sy had gone up top with the others. Then I saw the line." Hubie stopped and took a breath. His face blotched with patches of red, and he spoke in tortured breaths.

Cameron closed her eyes. "Don't say any more."

But he kept on. "The line was bouncing out of the water. Something big on it. One of Sy's sneakers was on the deck." Hubie began to cry, muffled sounds that tore his throat and shook his body. "My fault, Cameron. If I weren't such a stupid son-of-a-bitch I'd have been there to help him. Instead I was down below eating a goddamn baloney sandwich."

Hubie blew his nose. "I couldn't talk to Lynne about it. I was too wrapped up in my own misery I couldn't feel for anyone else. She blamed herself—if she hadn't made a move on Sy, none of this would have happened. It wasn't her fault. It was mine." Hubie paused and twirled his finger. "We went round and round till we were ready to kill each other." The carefree jokester with the baby face and booming voice was gone. In his place sat an overweight, middle-aged wreck.

"I'm sorry, Cameron. Seeing that old picture of Sy set me off and I'm sorry about what I said to Lynne. Sy didn't have any girlfriends. That didn't keep Lynne from being crazy about him."

Cameron turned away and looked toward the river. At that moment, she hated Hubie with such intensity that she wanted to scratch his eyes out, set dogs on him. Nothing was cruel enough to pay him back for this pain he was causing her. Could she ever erase the picture of Sy dangling at the end of the line? Hubie had dumped his burden of guilt on her, and now he'd go home and tell Maggie that his conscience was clear. Well, fuck him.

"What about that picture?" she asked, holding her voice in check.

Hubie's head jerked. "Who cares about an old picture? I'm talking about Sy getting killed."

He slumped in his chair. "I'm sorry. Didn't mean to bite your head off. That was a woman Sy dated when he was at BU. I met her couple of times when I went up there to see him. A real kook. Pretty. Crazy about Sy. Nothing to it as far as Sy was concerned."

Cameron believed him. He didn't have the strength to lie. Nothing to it, she thought. Just a beautiful son he'd never known existed.

"We've all been living with too many secrets. Let's go," she said.

Cameron barely had time to get home when she looked outside to see Lynne's red Bonneville pull into the driveway. There would be no escaping her. Lynne opened the screen door and walked in.

"You're about the last person I want to see right now. I just left Hubie. He told me everything about the country club and Sy's death the next day."

Lynne stopped, wide-eyed, startled. "Why is he bringing that up now?"

"That picture of Sy brought out guilt he's lived with all these years. Maggie told him he needed to get Sy's death off his chest."

"For Christ sakes, Cameron, Hubie's crazy. He couldn't have saved Sy even if he'd been standing beside him." Lynne dropped to the floor, pulling her legs under her. "And nothing happened that night at the Country Club. I saw Sy alone on the terrace. I went over and put my arms around him and said let's dance. That's all. Hubie came flying out accusing us of sleeping together. He was so damn jealous. Accused me of sleeping with half the men in Hobetown, as if anyone in their right mind would want to." Lynne laughed, trying to break the tension.

Cameron closed her eyes and turned away. "Why didn't you tell me?"

"There was nothing to tell." Lynne jumped to her feet and began pacing. "Don't listen to Hubie. He'll never get over Sy's death even if it wasn't his fault."

"Don't talk about it anymore." Cameron sighed. "You can do some stupid things, but I don't believe trying to steal Sy was one of them."

"Jesus, this is awful. He shouldn't have done that to you."

"It makes me wonder what else I don't know," Cameron said.

Lynne covered her face with her hands. After a moment she rose and walked to the door.

"This has been a horrible week. I'm going home and get drunk."

BIG MIKE

Michael had barely spoken since they boarded the plane home. Big Mike guessed that more than lack of sleep silenced him. He gave Michael a nudge. "You're mighty quiet. What you thinking about?"

"That you might be right."

"About what?"

"Genes carry memories."

Big Mike removed his glasses and rubbed his eyes. "How come you're thinking about that?"

"Melungeons and Middle Eastern diseases. How they're all connected. Remember when I was fifteen and Mom took me to that past life regression at the center?"

Big Mike bristled. He remembered all too well. Some of that stuff was okay, but she'd gone too far that time. When he found out what Margaret had done they'd gotten into such an argument that she'd threatened to take Michael and move out. The tension passed, but he let her know he didn't want anything like that to happen again. Michael remained moody for a long time after that and kept waking up with bad dreams.

"The shaman hypnotized the group and took us through different incarnations. Like watching a movie. All of a sudden I was looking at a man dressed in rich-looking robes, turban, beard, standing on a balcony, looking over an ancient city, like I'd imagine Constantinople would have looked. The balcony was connected to a room where a woman lay in bed holding a baby. Crazy thing was that I didn't know whether I was the sad-looking man, the sad-looking woman in bed, or the baby, but I knew I was one of them, and something horrible had happened in that room. Scared the hell out of me. When they brought us out of the hypnosis, I couldn't detach myself from that scene. Felt like I'd been drugged. My brain was so scrambled I was afraid I'd never get back into my own body. Must be how people feel who think they've seen a ghost or a UFO." Michael explained.

"She shouldn't have done that, and I told her so."

"I never told Mom, but that same shaman came back the next year, and I went to see him. Cool guy. Lived in the jungle in Brazil. Said what I'd experienced was a connection to the earth's force that binds everything together—planet, humans, animals—all the knowledge in the universe, past and future. He called it The Spark. Said man passes it from one generation to the next, but it's buried in the part of the brain that modern man doesn't use. He didn't understand genes, but he described the same thing you did."

"Spark, huh? Did you ask him why it scared you so bad?"

"He said some past life experience is so powerful it could work its way into your conscious mind. That's what schizophrenia was—break through of past life trauma. Said he could cure it if people would listen."

"Did it make you feel better?"

"Yeah, demystified it. Mom puts such a sinister spin on all that stuff. I stopped thinking about it."

Big Mike looked out the window at the thick bank of clouds. "You think that's where the FMF gene came from? That fellow standing on the balcony?"

"I don't know, but Mom does."

"You're full of surprises. Thought you were sitting here daydreaming about where you were last night."

"Kinda late when I got in, wasn't it. But how would you know. Heard you snoring from the parking lot."

"She's quite a girl," Big Mike said.

"She's a great girl. We just sat and talked and before I knew it, it was three o'clock. It's like I've known her all my life. Never met anyone like her."

"I'm not trying to mind your business, but you better be thinking about what you're doing.

Looking at a fork in the road for sure."

"I know," Michael said. "I don't feel like the same person who came to Newman's Ridge. I'm not even mad at Stephanie any more. It's like that happened to someone else.

"You've got a great future with her daddy's law firm. That's not happening to someone else."

Michael stretched his long legs into the aisle and pushed back his seat. "Last week I would have told you that being with his law firm was the most exciting possibility I could imagine. Now, I'm not so sure."

"Because of a pretty little mountain girl?"

"Partly, but she's not just a pretty little mountain girl."

"Uh huh."

"She has a three-year-old daughter. Planned to get married when she graduated from college, but she got pregnant a couple months before the wedding. When her boyfriend found out, he took off with a buddy for California and didn't return until the baby was born, ready to get married. She told him to hit the road."

Big Mike nodded. "Good for her."

"She got a student loan and enrolled in graduate school. Said that experience taught her that she had to take care of herself. She's smart. Going to research the Pattersons for me."

"Is there a Melungeon connection?"

"Yeah. I told her about the Indian grandmother. Said she's run across the name many times. She's sort of an expert on those inherited Mediterranean diseases. Her brother had Behcet Syndrome when he was a teenager. None of the doctors diagnosed it, and it went untreated. He's nearly blind. That's what got her interested."

"Has she seen other people with FMF?"

"Plenty."

Big Mike looked across at his grandson and wished he could think of something to say that would stop the twisting and turning going on in that good-looking head, pulling him into new territory. Dangerous territory. "Don't tell your mother any of this. And think about what you're doing before you make a decision."

Michael nodded, but Big Mike knew he might as well save his breath. His grandson, head of every class he attended, honest, trustworthy and as close to him as his own heartbeat, would do what he felt was the right thing. When he made his decision, no one could change his mind.

Thursday, September 19

CAMERON

Cameron found Marsha lettering the wall cards for the Selig exhibit they'd hung the previous day. She handed Cameron two slips of paper. "Someone named Thelma called and said Callie and Nell had gone to the Ramada. Here's her phone number." Marsha waited for an explanation. Cameron didn't respond, and she returned to her calligraphy.

Cameron looked out the window at the motel, visible above the treetops four blocks away. What were those girls up to?

The other message was from Lynne wanting to take her to lunch. She tossed both pieces of paper in the wastebasket.

"Ms. Ernie stopped by a little while ago," Marsha added. "Said to tell you she's decided to go to the Ramada if the storm's going to hit, so don't worry about her. She can get there by herself."

"Did she sound like she meant it?"

"No."

LYNNE

Lynne spent the morning organizing sketches. Now that her show was down she needed to get back to work, but Cameron's words, "Wonder what else I don't know?" had dogged every step she'd taken since then.

She'd been waiting for the right moment to tell Cameron about Mark and confess to having sex with him, but after what Hubie had said about her coming on to Sy, that moment was slipping away. Goddamn Hubie.

Right away she should have told Cameron what had happened in Atlanta six months ago. She'd intended to drive straight to Cameron's house as soon as she got home and blurt out the whole sordid thing, but she lost her nerve. After Mark left, there didn't seem to be any need to talk about it.

It happened when she'd gone to Atlanta to deliver paintings. The gallery owner had given her a hard time about his commissions. He thought artists should work for nothing. They'd been taking thirty percent, and now they wanted forty. She'd left angry and in need of a drink.

Lynne believed that it must have been luck,

bad luck, that made her walk into the hotel bar and spot Mark at a table hanging over some young, sexy thing. If he hadn't seen her, she'd have turned and gotten out of there, but it was too late. Their eyes met and they exchanged a nod. She took a stool at the bar. Minutes later he was beside her.

"This is a nice surprise," he said. "Let me buy you a drink."

"I wouldn't want to take you away from Lolita."

"She's got other things to do. I'd rather sit here with you anyway."

The drinks became two, then three, and by the time she knew she'd had too much her head was spinning. Mark paid the tab and walked her to the elevator. Her intention was to say thanks and leave him in the lobby, but when the door opened he guided her inside.

"Where are you going?" she asked.

Mark laughed a deep throaty sound and leaned down and kissed her on the mouth, running his hands down her back, pulling her against his body.

The elevator stopped and Mark followed her into the hall. "Key," he said, holding out his hand.

"No way." But she reached in her pocket.

In seconds he had her on the bed, saying how happy he could make her, removing her clothes. She should have yelled, screamed and kicked, made him leave, but she didn't. His hands found all the right spots. She let it happen.

After that, whenever she ran into Cameron and Mark, she made an excuse to get away. Cameron couldn't understand why she'd taken such a sudden dislike to him, but Lynne would only say that three's a crowd. She couldn't tell Cameron about Mark and the girl in the bar without implicating herself. She grudgingly held her silence.

CAMERON

Cameron looked out the front window and saw Callie and Nell coming down the street, gesturing to each other and swinging their arms excitedly. She could hear their high-pitched laughter a half-block away.

"Hello, Callie," Cameron said, extending her hand in welcome. "It's good to see you. You're looking well." Callie had on flowered pants with matching blouse, her hair and make-up carefully done. She flashed a grin as big as the sky behind her and patted Nell's shoulder. "Nell and me has finally met."

"I guess it's time to start sharing her." Cameron forced a smile. "Would you like to have a seat? I've got some drinks in the back."

"Drinks?" Callie asked.

"Cokes."

"Oh. That'd be fine."

Nell faced Cameron. "We need to talk."

"I'm getting ready to lock up. Have a seat in the office."

Cameron took her time. From the conspiratorial glances they exchanged, they were up to something.

Nell's hair, blue-black and plastered against her head with a gelatinous substance, glistened under the overhead light. No more charcoal-ringed eyes and black lipstick. She wore a jean skirt and tee shirt, cowboy boots. Altogether a modest look for Nell.

"Callie's decided to stay in Hobetown. We're going to get an apartment." Nell smiled at Callie who nodded in agreement. "And we're going into business."

"Business?" Cameron repeated, shocked.

"Thelma, my grandmother, is making a lot of money cleaning houses for all the new waterfront communities going up. She's hired a couple of Mexican women to help, and they've got more work than they can handle."

Callie interrupted. "Ma says if someone opened a reliable cleaning service they'd make a killing."

"You want to clean houses?" Cameron asked, incredulous. Nell didn't like to clean her own room.

"Not us," Nell snapped back. "We're going to hire the women."

Callie spoke up. "With Nell's college education she knows how to do the business part, and I'll manage the women. Ma's got a bunch of names that want to work."

"The biggest problem is getting them to the job. Most of the women don't have transportation.

Nell laid out the business plan. "We need a van and an office where we can set up the phone. What we want is for you to sign over the rest of my college money, and we'll get started. It's mine, anyway." Nell cast her eyes toward the floor then looked up, defiant. "You'd probably be glad to get rid of me."

"Nell," Cameron replied, embarrassed by her daughter's hostile remark "You've drawn out almost all the money in that trust."

Nell jumped to her feet. "I knew you'd say that. My father left me enough to attend a four-year college. I've only been one year."

"I know," Cameron reasoned. "But we've been paying colleges that you keep dropping out of. I don't think there's five thousand dollars left."

Nell paced the room. "It's not my fault the stupid schools offer nothing I want."

"We still had to pay them."

"I have an investor who'll finance our business, but I don't have the money yet," Nell said. "I can pay it back later. Thelma said ten, maybe twelve thousand dollars would set everything up."

"Then why not go to the bank and borrow the money? All of you can sign the loan," Cameron said.

Callie sat up straight and shot a look at Nell. "You didn't say nothing about no bank loan."

"It's my money. My father left it for me," Nell demanded.

Cameron crossed her arms over her chest. "We need to discuss this further and now's not the time."

Callie looked at her watch. "Let's get out of here. I want to go to the cafe." She walked to the door and motioned for Nell to follow.

Cameron watched them hurry down the street, then picked up the phone and called Thelma.

"Nell and Callie just left. Said they're going to open a business with you. They want ten thousand dollars. What's going on?"

"Lord Jesus. I told them to wait 'til Nell had the money, then we'd all sit down and talk."

"What money are you talking about?"

"Nell said she's getting ten thousand dollars in a couple of weeks. Figured you knew about it."

"I don't."

"This ain't good. Don't you give them any money. Least not as long as Callie's got anything to do with it. Hate to say it, but all Callie's been talking about since she and Nell met is getting hold of that money."

"Is Callie moving to Hobetown? They said they're getting an apartment together."

Cameron heard a quick intake of breath. "I should never have called her. Should have let you and Nell work out whatever was bothering ya'll. Don't give them girls any money and get that credit card back. Callie said it has a twenty-thousand dollar limit."

"Nell needs money, but I can call the bank and put a cap on it. Other than that, I don't know what else to do."

"Pray," Thelma said. "Pray that Callie goes back to Florida and Nell don't get hurt too bad. She's a sweet girl. Smart, too. Me and James really took to her."

"I'm glad, but she's all I've got and I don't want to lose her."

"I wouldn't worry about that. You raised Nell right. Sometimes you have to wait to see the rewards of that, but it'll come. I've raised enough children to know."

"Hope you're right. I feel better knowing you're around."

Cameron phoned the Ramada. The desk clerk said that Nell and her friend had gone to the cafe. "Would you give her a message to call Cameron?"

She hung up wondering why she didn't say *call your mother*.

MICHAEL

Michael had planned to go into the office Thursday after he returned from Newman's Ridge, but when the alarm clock went off, he rolled over and pulled the covers over his head. They weren't expecting him. He was supposed to be in Maine on vacation. Steff had left a message. Since her week was ruined, she and her mother were going to New York shopping. He needed to talk to her. The sooner the better, but he'd have to wait until she got back.

He tried to go back to sleep, but Big Mike's words kept running through his mind. "You've reached a fork in the road." Big Mike was right, and he intended to choose the one that didn't have Steff waiting at the end. He didn't love her. He'd fallen in love with the access she provided to all the things he thought would make him happy, things other people seemed to want. Haley made that clear. If he really loved Steff, he'd have been hurt, but what he really felt was anger. He was mad as hell that she so casually betrayed him.

Knowing how Steff operated, she'd leave him dangling till he saw her Monday at the office. She'd be cool, suggest they have a drink after work, where she'd remind him what an unappreciative asshole he was. He knew the drill. He'd be forgiven and they'd end up back at her apartment in bed.

He had another plan. Monday, when they were both back at work, he'd ask her to meet him in his office after the others left. He didn't want alcohol or the bed in the next room to distract from what had to be done. She'd be furious and throw him out, and he'd call Mr. Curtis the next morning and resign. Wade Curtis would be disappointed. Already he'd begun dropping hints about turning the practice over to his daughter and her future husband. Mr. Curtis was a good man, and he hated to let him down.

Then he'd be out of work. He could get another job in Hartford if he wanted to stay here, but probably not. Boston was out of the question. He might like Washington. Just where Haley fit into the picture he didn't know. There'd be plenty of time to think about that later. Right now he needed to start the medication and get healthy. He'd give the doctor a call.

The rest of the morning he cleaned the apartment and watched TV. At two o'clock he walked to the corner and bought a pizza that he washed down with a beer. When he got back to the apartment he fell across the bed and slept until the phone woke him at six. He rolled over but didn't answer it.

He waited until ten o'clock to call Haley.

She told him she'd been busy all day working on files for Melungeon Cousins, and researching the Patterson line. She'd accumulated information about the family, but it wasn't complete. He hinted at another visit to Vardy to gather her material, but she didn't respond.

When he hung up he turned on the Weather Channel to get a report of the hurricane. The hope that it would veer out to sea looked slim, and the latest predictions had it making landfall along the South Carolina coast Sunday. Should he call Cameron? He wished he knew what she planned to do if the hurricane hit Hobetown.

The phone rang again. That would be his mother.

"You been watching TV?" Margaret asked.

"I'm watching it now."

"That hurricane looks bad, doesn't it?"

"Uh-huh."

"That's where you were last week, isn't it?"

"Yes, Mother. That's where I was."

"You working this weekend?"

"I'm still on vacation. Thinking about going to the shore."

"Glad to hear that. You need a rest. Stephanie loves the beach, doesn't she?"

"Yes, she does."

Friday, September 20

CAMERON

"I'll be back before the guests arrive," Cameron assured Marsha and hurried out the back door. "It won't take me long to change."

Blackened clouds tumbled on the southern horizon, and a light rain began to fall. The stale air being pushed ahead of the storm felt heavy on her skin. Sunday, they'd said. It wasn't going to hit until Sunday. It felt closer.

She planned to take a quick shower and change into a pink silk shirt and black pants she'd bought for the opening. Before she left the house that morning she'd laid the clothes on the bed, along with a colorful scarf she might wear, and diamond stud earrings that Sy had given her their last Christmas.

Lynne said to wear her hair down and use a little more blush and blue mascara to brighten her eyes.

Cameron opened the door and stepped over a tee shirt Nell had dropped on the living room floor. She picked it up and walked into Nell's room. The closet door was open and most of her clothes were gone. How could Nell move out without telling her? Yesterday, Nell had left a message that she'd be spending the night with her grandparents, but she'd said nothing about leaving home. She wadded up the shirt and threw it on a chair.

Anger faded when she saw Mr. B, Nell's floppy-eared bunny and cherished companion since she was a toddler. The sight of the battered old rabbit lying on the pillow sent a pain through Cameron's chest. She closed her eyes and for a moment saw a happy little blonde-haired girl wearing her favorite shirt with the monkeys on the front, sitting on the bed, playing with her dolls.

Cameron sank to the floor, her head in her hands. She thought she'd be relieved when Nell left, but she only felt despair. And guilt. And failure. Her eyes burned with tears she fought to hold back. This was her fault. She should have tried harder.

When she returned to the gallery, Benjamin Selig, looking old and frail, sat in a chair by the front door. He'd been sick, he said, and if she didn't mind he'd just stay there and greet the people. Marsha watched the entrance, rubbing her hands, as the first guest pulled into the driveway.

*

"Where's your doctor friend?" Lynne asked.

She'd been watching the door all evening as she moved among the guests.

Cameron's face broke into a wide smile. "Right there."

Sanjay Rao, wearing that pink tie, and a diminutive older man, dressed like the Sikhs in the photographs, made their way through the crowd toward her.

"Cameron, I'd like you to meet my father, Bandar Rao." Bandar pressed his palms together in a *wai* greeting and then raised her hand to his lips.

"A pleasure to meet you," he said. "Thank you for letting my son bring me. I have been looking forward to this." His eyes twinkled as he looked around the room and came to rest on the photographs. "Oh, my," he exclaimed and crossed his hands over his heart. "This makes me homesick."

Dr. Rao turned to Cameron. "My father is visiting from India. I'm doing my best to keep him happy, but he's been trying to leave since he got off the plane."

The elder Rao gave a soft laugh and walked away to examine the photographs.

Dr. Rao turned to Cameron, "Please call me Sanjay. I'd feel more comfortable." He was poised to say more, but the elder Rao motioned from across the room, his turbaned head bobbing excitedly.

"Excuse me," he said. "My father's found something."

Cameron counted forty people; most were from Charleston, an hour's drive away. That was more than she'd expected and a good indication of a successful show, but there was too much talk of the hurricane. She worked the crowd, keeping an eye on Sanjay and his father, and watched as the pair discussed each scene in hushed tones. The scene of a country village held their attention. Bandar Rao spoke rapidly in Hindi, pointing out details. Cameron joined them.

"My father says this is a village in the district where he was born. It's in the North, in the mountains."

"It is very beautiful," Bandar said. "Haven't been there since I was a young man." He was lost for a moment in remembrances, and then said to Cameron, "What a wonderful surprise to find this here." He eyes shone.

Bandar turned to his son. "We must have this—and several others. I will feel more at home with these beautiful pictures than those you have hanging in my room." He patted Sanjay's arm. "His paintings are interesting, but these bring comfort to an old man far from home."

"I give him the peace and quiet he always asked for and now he doesn't know what to do with it," Sanjay teased.

Bandar nodded. "Foolish creatures, aren't we? Always wanting what we don't have. My son's home is beautiful and serene. Have you seen his art collection?"

"No."

"Then you must. Do you like Indian food?"

"I'm not sure I've ever tasted the real thing."

"We shall remedy that. I brought Yash, my cook, with me." He winked at Sanjay. "Never trust the kitchen of a bachelor son."

Bandar ignored Sanjay's frown. "Next week, when the hurricane is past, you must join us. We'll send a car for you."

Lynne joined them, edging her bare shoulder, tattooed with a lacy spider web, between the men. Her long red hair fell around her shoulders, her eyebrows outlined in tiny green crystals. "Hi. I'm Lynne Earl," she said, extending her hand to Sanjay. "That's my painting you looked at in the back of the gallery—what's left from the show Cameron just took down."

Cameron wished Lynne didn't look so good and flashed her a warning frown.

"I'm interested in your work, Ms. Earl." Sanjay said, "I'd like to see more of it."

"Perhaps Cameron can bring you to my studio," Lynne replied.

Sanjay nodded and the men moved on to the next photograph.

Lynne whispered, "Otherness."

Gusts of rain increased, and the crowd grew restless. She heard the perfunctory exchanges of conversation with the photographer, praise for the collection and promises to return next week. The crowd thinned. Cameron relaxed when she counted red dots on four woodcuts and six photographs.

The Raos headed toward the door, preparing to leave, and Sanjay took Cameron aside. "I haven't seen my father in such a good mood since he arrived. Thank you. And he'd like very much for you to come to lunch." He laughed softly. "Give him and Yash something to do."

"I'd love that."

Sanjay shifted from one foot to the other. Cameron had never seen him at a loss for words. "This is not the place, I know, but we got distracted Tuesday and didn't discuss the referral. I've spoken to Dr. Elston about taking you as a patient. I highly recommend him...."

Cameron pulled back, shocked. "You don't want to see me again?"

Sanjay took her arm and stared down into her face, "Of course I want to see you. That's the point."

She could think of nothing to say, and for the first time in years she blushed. Before she could regain her composure the door opened. Callie walked in, Nell behind her. "Well, here we are. Come to see the show," Callie called out.

Cameron looked up at Sanjay and squeezed her eyes closed. Nell's hair, spiked into carrot-colored cones, shot out in every direction. Rows of rhinestones pierced both ears. Black mascara encircled her dark eyes making them appear startlingly large. Her cutoff jean skirt barely covered her thong panties. Under Nell's plaid jacket, Cameron couldn't read all the lettering on her tee shirt, stretched across her thin chest, but saw enough to hope others couldn't either. Black and yellow striped knee socks springing from laced-up combat boots completed the costume. Except for the hair, and boots, Callie was a modified copy of her daughter.

Callie glanced around the room, hostile. "This is just a bunch of Kodaks. Thought you said this was an art show."

Nell eased Callie toward the back of the gallery.

"They're photographs of India. Guy who took them is a Pulitzer Prize winner," Cameron heard Nell say.

Callie frowned at the unfamiliar words and pulled away, bumping into a chair, then steadied herself and looked around the room.

"Bullshit," she said. "You think I don't know real art when I see it." Callie circled the room, glancing at each photograph until she reached the woodcuts. "Wouldn't call this stuff art either. Looks like something you'd buy at the mall."

"Would you like me to stay?" Sanjay whispered to Cameron. His eyes followed Callie around the room. "Yash is waiting outside. He can take father home."

Cameron nodded. "Somebody needs to get her out of here."

Benjamin Selig was making his way to the door, accompanied by several guests. "I really must go." He hugged Cameron. "Thanks. Lovely party. I'll come next week when things are quiet."

Sanjay had cornered Callie, talking to her about the photographs. Lynne, watching from across the room, stepped forward. "Come on girls, party's over. I'll give you a ride."

"Take us to the Ramada," Nell said.

"I'm not ready to go. Haven't even had a drink." Callie reached in her pocketbook, pulled out a pack of cigarettes, and turned to Nell. "You said we'd have fun tonight. When's it gonna start?"

Nell took the pack from Callie and stuffed it in her pocket. "Stay if you want. I'm leaving."

Callie put her hands on her hips and held her ground a moment before she followed Lynne to the back door where she turned and threw a disgusted look at Cameron.

When everyone was gone, Sanjay helped Cameron pick up wine glasses, while the caterer, eager to get away, packed the hors d'oeuvre trays.

"What about the exhibit?" he asked. "Are you going to leave it hanging?"

"Marsha is meeting me at nine in the morning. We'll decide then whether to pack it up. Now there're saying the storm might go out to sea."

"I'll be glad to help you. There aren't that

many pieces."

"I'd rather not move them unless it's necessary. Insurance problems. We should have plenty of time in the morning. Besides, you've helped enough by staying here. That could have gotten ugly."

"Your friend did the right thing to take the girls out of here."

"Your father must wonder what's going on."

"He's accustomed to family drama. The Rao complex in Delhi is a small village of confusion. This will make him feel more at home."

She was unnerved, not just from the disruption Nell and Callie had created, but from the way Sanjay acted toward her.

"You'll need a ride home," she said.

"Yash can come back for me. If you don't have plans, I'd like to take you to dinner. Is there a restaurant nearby?"

"There's a cafe three blocks away. More of a bar than a restaurant, but we can get fresh fish and chips." The invitation was so unexpected she looked away; afraid he'd see the excitement in her eyes.

"Sounds perfect."

*

Captain Ben's Cafe didn't usually get busy on Friday nights till ten, but the locals, the ones not boarding up windows and making preparations for the storm, had gathered around the bar to watch the weather reports on TV and have a few beers. Steve pointed to a table when he saw Cameron and Sanjay making their way through the boisterous crowd.

All the anxiety Cameron felt at being with Sanjay faded in minutes. He seemed relaxed, comfortable among men who looked and acted so differently from him. She asked him about growing up in Delhi, and he described life in a compound of aunts, uncles, countless cousins, servants and pets. *Arabian Nights* couldn't sound more exotic. His mother had died recently, which was one reason for his father's visit. Sanjay hoped to cheer him up, but so far he hadn't been successful. Life in America was too different, and he was homesick.

"I grew up hearing how all he wanted was a moment's peace," Sanjay laughed. "Now that he has it, he's bored to death. But I understand; he misses my mother."

When he asked Cameron to describe her childhood, all she could think of was the 4th of July parade that marched through the business district each year, the high school band leading the homemade floats and filling the air with sour notes. There was always nervous competition among the young girls to ride in the lead car, a classic convertible brought out of storage especially for the occasion. Three times Cameron had won the honor. Sanjay listened, laughing at her description of Mr. Johnson's mule, Wilbur, decorated in red, white and blue streamers, pulling a Revolutionary War cannon. How Wilbur always stopped halfway down River Road to take a dump. The parade wasn't complete without it.

Yash was waiting in the parking lot when Sanjay walked Cameron to her car.

"I'll call you tomorrow. Okay?" he said.

"Okay."

Saturday, September 21

CAMERON

An electrical arc flashed through the bedroom window and brought Cameron leaping to her feet. Outside, a transformer sizzled under the blow of a fallen ancient oak. Sparks flashed across the street.

The wind came in blasts. Driving rain sounded like buckshot hitting the windows. Cameron pulled on a pair of jeans and grabbed her keys. She looked at her watch; seven o'clock. She'd stop and get something to eat on the way to meet Marsha.

Quikie Mart, already boarded up, smelled of fresh coffee and bacon. A group of Latino men with their eyes fixed on the TV had gathered to watch the weather report. They exchanged nervous glances while they waited for someone to translate. Cameron paused long enough to hear that Hilda was expected to make landfall south of Hobetown around one o'clock that afternoon with sustained winds of 120 miles per hour and gusts up to 150.

The warning was out: Be off the roads by ten o'clock this morning.

"Oh, my God," Cameron said to the clerk behind the counter. "When did that happen?"

"During the night. Damn thing just took off. It's coming straight at us. They're calling for everyone to find a shelter. Churches is taking folks in."

Cameron pointed to the group huddled in front of the TV. "Do they know that?"

"They'll figure it out. Boss just called and said to shut the place down. Electricity's about to go out, so get what you want."

Without waiting for coffee, she ran to her car. If she hurried she'd have time to pack up the exhibit then go straight to the Ramada and wait it out. She couldn't expect Marsha to come out in this weather.

Cameron pulled up to the gallery and looked across the street. A light shone through the shuttered windows. Ms. Ernie would never leave one burning if she wasn't home.

The wind had picked up, whipping rain in horizontal slices. Cameron pulled her soaked raincoat over her head and waited for the gust to subside before she dashed across the street, up the slippery stairs and pounded on the door.

Ms. Ernie's head appeared around the dining room door. Seeing Cameron, she rushed to open the door."

"Good Lord, child, what are you doing

here?"

"I've come to get you."

Ms. Ernie pulled her inside. "There's no need. I'm fine right here."

"You're not. You've got to get out of here."

"Do you know how many hurricanes I've lived through? My father and mother and baby brother sat right here through the worst storm ever to hit the coast. Homes gone all around us. Not this one. My father built ours to stay."

There was no point in arguing that houses withstood hurricanes indiscriminately—a brick mansion could be reduced to rubble while a nearby tenant shack remained standing.

"I have plenty of oil lamps, water and food." Ms. Ernie pointed to ice chests along the wall. "Enough for the neighborhood. Don't worry about me. I'm just fine. Go home while you can get there."

"There's mandatory evacuation. They won't rescue anyone."

Ms. Ernie pushed Cameron toward the door. "Honey, I'll see you when the storm's over. Now, go."

Short Cut Billy, holding a piece of plastic over his head, had taken shelter under the porch.

"You shouldn't be here," Cameron said.

"Come to check on Ms. Ernie."

"She's okay. Determined to stay."

The wind had momentarily died down, but Billy swayed and Cameron caught the stench of cheap wine. "You better get to a shelter."

"Naw," he grinned. "I've got something here that'll keep me warm." He patted his jacket.

"Warm isn't safe."

He pulled his baseball cap down. "Ain't never gone to no shelter, and I'm still here. Gonna slip under the house, out of the wind, be like a bug in a rug."

Cameron gave up and dashed back across the street just as a dark sedan pulled into the gallery driveway. The window rolled down and Sanjay called out, but his words blew away, swallowed by the wind. He motioned for her to get in the car.

"Thought I'd find you here," he said.

"I have to pack up the show. Take it someplace safe."

"Will it fit in my car?"

"I think so."

"Then, let's get it. What about the paintings in your bins?"

Cameron threw up her hands. "I can't pack up everything. They're replaceable. Benjamin's collection isn't."

While Sanjay bubble-wrapped the prints, Cameron tried to phone Nell, but there was no response at the Ramada. She called Lynne and got an immediate answer.

"Sanjay's here, I'm going to his house," Cameron said. "Are you going to the Ramada?"

"Buddy's coming to get me."

"Check on Nell. . . ." Before she could finish the sentence, the phone crackled and Cameron heard nothing more but static.

They stacked the photographs and woodcuts in the car, running back and forth between blasts of driving rain, both of them soaked. When they finished, Sanjay waited with the motor running while Cameron hurried through her desk gathering phone numbers, check book, her client index.

Before she closed the door, she looked around the gallery. She never thought that the one thing in her life she could depend on to make her happy could be gone. For an instant, the image of Sy flashed across her mind. He was holding one of his paintings; a look of childish gratitude on his face because he'd just sold his first watercolor.

"I'm sorry, Sy," she said. "There's nothing I can do."

LYNNE

Lynne yelled "Good luck!" into the sputtering phone and hung up, cut off before she could ask what brought Dr. Rao to Cameron's rescue.

Looking around her studio, she wished someone was there to help her. All the canvases needed to be wrapped and stored in the brick well house, and she only had a couple of hours before Buddy would come to get her.

She'd squeezed in the last canvas, and was struggling with the lock when his red pickup pulled in the driveway.

"Hurry up," he yelled. "I gotta get back."

"Come help me," she called out over the roar of the wind. "It won't stay shut."

Buddy leaped from the truck and grabbed a ladder out of the back. He dragged it across the yard, pushed one end against the door and stomped the other into the ground. With it secure, they ran for the truck.

Lynne's house was less than a mile from the Ramada, and before they'd gone half the distance a tree crashed across the road, smothering the pickup in leaves and branches.

"Get out," Buddy yelled, and he set out running with Lynne trailing behind, ducking her head against each new blast of wind.

Buddy and Lynne ran through the side door of the Ramada, wet and breathless, to find Hobetown residents taking refuge in the lobby, the only place with electricity thanks to the new generator. Windows facing the river, the direction from which the storm would come, had been boarded-up, and unless something catastrophic happened, everyone would be safe.

Lynne looked across the parking lot behind the building and saw a figure running through the rain toward them. The next moment Nell burst through the back door, soaked, out of breath and looking terrified.

"Where's Callie?" She ran past Lynne toward the people gathered in the lobby.

Lynne starred after her. "What are you doing out in this storm?"

Without answering, Nell ran back and disappeared up the stairs.

Fifteen minutes later, the elevator door opened, and she and Callie got out, tugging their suitcases.

"Where's Buddy?" Nell cried. "I need to pay my bill."

"Are you crazy?" Lynne shrieked.

"We've got to get out of here." Callie backed off, wringing her hands.

"Buddy's upstairs checking the windows."

Nell grabbed her bags and ran toward the door to the parking lot. "Come on, Callie. I'll pay 'em later."

Just then the local radio station they'd listened to all morning signed off the air with the final report that the estimated landfall for Hilda should be around one-thirty, twenty miles south of Hobetown. If that happened the eye wouldn't pass over them, but the hurricane's treacherous northern winds would and they'd be in danger until it moved inland. Nothing to do but hunker down, open a few beers and wait it out.

CAMERON

Cocooned inside the car, Cameron crouched low in the seat. Sanjay struggled to hold the road, swerving to avoid branches and debris. Any minute Cameron expected a tree to crash down on them. They met a few cars, mostly pickups, and exchanged worried looks with their drivers.

"You can relax," Sanjay said, and turned off the road. "There's my house."

Ahead, on a rise above the bay, Cameron saw a wall surrounding a large white, two-story box, boarded up with plywood. She guessed the entire structure was made of poured concrete, like houses she'd seen in slick home magazines. The trees lining the driveway swung their branches frantically, flailing and slapping the car as it passed between them. Flashes of color from destroyed flowerbeds flew through the air.

Sanjay pulled into the garage and closed the door.

"This feels like a bank vault," Cameron said, emitting a thankful sigh.

"Everything is safe but the garden—the one thing my father enjoyed. He's going to be upset when he comes back. Yash has taken him to

Atlanta."

They entered the house through the garage door into a world that, at first glance, seemed more like a museum than a home. Polished concrete floors reflected the stark white walls hung with recognizable works of art. The furnishings were sparse but notable: Eames chairs, Chihuly lamps, oriental carpets, and artful pieces of wood sculpted into tables. Cameron spotted a Nevelson sculpture.

"Aren't you afraid to leave this art here?"

"Where would I take it? Of course, it's insured."

"Even so." She looked around. "I feel like I'm in a gallery."

"You sound like my father." Sanjay turned on more lights. "It's really quite comfortable. We do have a generator so we won't be without electricity." He took her hand and led her across the living room. "Let me show you the guest room where you can wash up."

Cameron looked around the beautifully appointed guest room: thick carpet, silk drapery, colors in shades of sand. She found it restful, what she'd expect in his home. She'd spent her entire life in a two hundred year-old house with chipped paint and sagging floors and found this perfection intimidating. A beautifully executed portrait of an Indian woman hung on the wall opposite the bed. She wore western clothes and held a book on her lap. Cameron felt those piercing eyes follow her as she moved about the room.

Without clean clothes and makeup, there was little she could do about her appearance. She joined Sanjay in the kitchen where he'd gone to make sandwiches, and watched him a moment before he looked up and smiled at her. This was all so new and unexpected. She wasn't sure what to say.

"Relax. There's nothing we can do but wait it out," he said. "I'll take you home later."

Cameron took her sandwich to the living room and curled up on the sofa.

"Stretch out," he said. "It's going to be a long afternoon." With a few clicks on a remote, doors opened and a TV emerged from behind the wall.

Although objects bounced off the roof and hit the shutters with a crash, the outside world was visible only on TV.

"I feel like Alice in Wonderland peeping up through the rabbit hole. A splendid rabbit hole at that." She could feel Sanjay's eyes. She didn't trust herself to meet them, so she concentrated on the news reporters wrapped in slickers being tossed about on every beach town along the coast. It looked like Hobetown would be spared the worst of the storm's wrath, but the barrier islands to the south lay directly in Hilda's path. The storm surge was expected to reach twenty feet. Houses she'd vacationed in all her life along Lighthouse Island couldn't withstand a direct assault. Those beautiful old cottages with their lacy fretwork and wide porches wouldn't be there for another generation to enjoy. Her eyes filled with tears. She was tired of losing; tired of saying goodbye to things she loved.

Sanjay put his hand on her shoulder. "You okay?"

Cameron tried to smile. "I was thinking about Lighthouse Island."

A loud crash brought Cameron to her feet, and she looked at Sanjay for reassurance.

He wrapped his arms around her, drawing her to him. She could feel his heart beating, like hers, too fast. The wind had become a steady howl, drowning out their voices so they remained silent, holding each other, flinching at the sound of flying debris hitting the house. The shutters on the large windows began to budge. She watched them strain. If they tore loose, the glass would explode. She clung to Sanjay.

"Maybe we better go to the other side of the house. I'm sure the shutters will hold, but just in case." He led her to his bedroom. "I must confess I've never been through a hurricane."

The bed was unmade, just as he'd left it that morning. Cameron sat on the floor, leaned against it and covered her ears. Sanjay sank beside her, holding her next to him.

Although Cameron would later say it seemed like hours they sat together, rigid with fear, it took less than twenty minutes for the fast-moving storm to pass. One minute it sounded like the house would blow apart and then, silence. "It's over," she said.

"Just like that?" Sanjay asked, getting to his feet. "So quickly?"

He took her hand, and like sleepwalkers they moved through the house to the garage. Sanjay raised the door, took a few steps and covered his eyes. His dock had disappeared. Only a few poles remained standing in the water. Tree limbs littered the driveway along with a sodden mattress and pieces of furniture from neighbors' houses.

Boats, some still intact, lay on the shore like cast-aside toys. Across the bay curtains flapped from shattered windows in a two-story home, the roof mostly missing. In every direction uprooted trees left gaping craters in the earth. An eerie quiet had overtaken the scene.

They walked around the property stopping to pick up a picture frame or kick aside a piece of building material. Inside the wall that protected the house, knee-deep debris buried the battered flower gardens.

Together they removed shutters from the kitchen and living room windows before an orphaned band of rain drove them inside. It was only minutes before it too was gone, hurrying to catch the mother storm, leaving behind an angry sky, but with patches of blue breaking through. Cameron watched as a tall pine slowly leaned to earth. "You won't be able to get the car out," she said. "A tree just fell across the driveway."

"My gardener lives a mile away. He'll be here in the morning and remove it. Do you mind spending the night?"

She didn't mind. "I'd feel better if I knew where Nell was and what's happened to Hobetown."

"We could walk out to the road and try to catch a ride, but I think it's best to stay here. You'll probably learn more by watching TV."

He was right. The roads would be impassible. There'd be no phones or electricity working in Hobetown. They settled back on the sofa to watch camera crews emerge from parked trucks and hotel lobbies to film the devastation along the coast. No camera crews showed up in Hobetown, but an airplane taking aerial shots reported that the worst damage to the town was along the waterfront business district. The Ramada looked unscathed. If Nell were there, she'd be safe.

When the pictures began to repeat, Sanjay turned off the TV and walked to the bar. "We need a break. Gin and tonic?"

Cameron reached across the coffee table and opened an inlaid wooden box she'd looked at earlier. "I'd rather have one of these." She picked up a hand-rolled reefer, resting on a nest of shredded marijuana.

Sanjay laughed. "You'll have to ask my father. They're his. He smokes one a day, in the evening before he prays."

This struck Cameron as amusing, and she put it back.

"I don't think he'll miss it. There're plenty more where this came from." He took the reefer from the box, lit it and handed it to her. "Father brought his whole kitchen with him. Don't ask me how he arranged it with customs, but the marijuana was part of the spices."

It had been years since Cameron smoked pot. She closed her eyes and let the forbidden weed work its magic. She blew a silvery stream into the air and moved closer to Sanjay. He lay back and pulled her to him. They finished the reefer. She ran her fingers across his lips.

"They're much too perfect for a man," she said, and leaned down and kissed them. In the soft light, his nearly black eyes looked murky, dulled by desire. He shifted and Cameron moved closer, easing her body across his legs, onto his chest. She unbuttoned his shirt and ran her hands under his arms. She could feel his erection against her leg. He tried to roll her under him, but she resisted and held him down. He pulled off her shirt, removed his.

"Let's take these off," he said and pulled down her jeans.

Cameron reached for the bulge in his trousers. He unbuckled his belt and she unzipped him, cupping him in her hand. Sanjay closed his eyes and moaned in pleasure. He felt beautiful to her. His penis was hard and thick and smooth as velvet. Emboldened by the marijuana, she smiled into his eyes as she let him slowly slide her body under him and enter her.

LYNNE

Lynne peeked through the Ramada's shutters at the streaks of clear sky, listening to make sure the silence was the calm after the storm, not the eye passing over. People headed for the doors, eager to see what was left of Hobetown.

One of the plate-glass windows had shattered when a tree fell against the building, but the damage to the motel was minimal compared to what they saw along the waterfront. Backs of buildings had been torn away. Most of the boardwalk lay in splinters. Furniture and tree trunks, regurgitated by the surging river, littered the cafe parking lot. Lynne recognized the hood of her car under the rubble. It would be days before they got it out.

Word soon reached the Ramada that Ms. Ernie was found lying in the yard, dead, her neck broken. It appeared she'd fallen through the railing on her porch. The departing townspeople heard the sad news and shook their heads. Poor Ms. Ernie.

Lynne wanted to go home, but River Road was closed to everyone until crews removed the carnage. Streets were too dangerous to drive with downed power lines and debris. A firefighter stopped by to say that neither her house nor Cameron's had sustained much damage other than a yard full of trash and tree limbs. He said it looked like her glassed-in studio was okay, but she wanted to see for herself. All she owned was in that house, and she didn't intend to leave it unprotected.

She wouldn't have electricity untill God knows when, but she had candles and lamps and she could manage.

At eight o'clock she called out to Buddy, who was mopping up water that continued to seep into the lobby, that River Road was open. If he wouldn't take her, she intended to walk home.

Dallas came through the door, dressed in a clean, dry shirt and uniform trousers.

"Looks like y'all got by all right," he said.

Buddy put the mop down and turned to Dallas. "Tell Lynne she can't walk home."

"Why you want to do that?" Dallas asked

"Need to check on my house before that Back Creek crowd does."

"I'll give you a ride."

Lynne looked at Buddy, expecting him to say never mind, he'd take her, but he shrugged and picked up his mop.

Lynne grabbed her handbag and followed Dallas to his car.

"Them young guys just don't know how to treat a woman," Dallas said and patted her behind.

The patrol car smelled of sweat and beer. She

rolled the window down. "Tell me about Ms. Ernie. What happened?"

"Broke her neck."

"I know that. How?"

"We're trying to find out."

Dallas drove to Short Street and pulled into Cameron's driveway

"Why are you coming here?" Lynne asked.

"Go check it out. See if she's in there."

She couldn't tell Dallas to check it out himself. If Cameron were inside, what would she do if she saw Dallas coming up her walk? The front door was locked. She could see no lamps or candles burning inside. She called out a couple of times before she returned to the car.

"Go around back," Dallas said.

"She's not here. Probably still at Dr. Rao's house."

"That colored fellow she was with Friday night."

"He's Indian."

"Same thing."

Lynne rolled her eyes. "You're disgusting."

"That's not what you said the last time you and me was…"

"Last time is right."

Dallas laughed and put his hand on her thigh, edging it higher as he leaned closer. "Aren't you getting tired of that little-boy stuff?"

"I'm doing just fine. Let's go."

Dallas backed the car out of the driveway

and headed toward River Road. "Ask your boyfriend who slips in the back room and spends the night with him after she gets off work."

"You don't know what you're talking about."

"Honey, I know everything that goes on in this town. I'm the police chief." His lips spread in a lascivious grin, and his hand eased higher up her thigh. "If I wasn't so busy tonight I'd come in, and me and you would…"

They'd reached the house. Lynne got out of the car and called over her shoulder. "Not on your life."

Sunday, September 22

CAMERON

Cameron woke before Sanjay and lay quietly, looking at the paintings and sculpture in the room, imagining how it would feel to belong here. She'd spent her life in a tiny town among people who lived in old houses much like hers, people with little curiosity about the outside world, artifacts of a way of life in its death throes. Looking around at Sanjay's world, Cameron realized that Hobetown wasn't just a place where she was born; it defined who she was. Her mind raced ahead to possibilities unimaginable twenty-four hours before. She was jumping the gun a bit, but what if she and Sanjay wanted a permanent relationship? Could he live in her house, the only dark-skinned Asian in Hobetown? Could she live in this concrete palace on top of a hill, with neighbors too far away to call if she needed help? Was Lynne right? Was it Sanjay she was attracted to, or was it the "otherness", as Lynne called it? But she felt safe with him, and for now, that was enough.

How her life had changed. Nine days ago Michael walked into her gallery. Callie appeared. Sanjay had become her lover. She'd lived seven years since Sy died with nothing more than an occasional hurricane threat to challenge her, and in nine days her life had changed forever.

Sanjay stirred and pulled her to him, kissing the soft skin of her neck. "Been awake long?"

"I was going to slip out of bed 'til I realized I don't have any clean clothes."

"Yash has some things in the guest room closet you can slip on, later."

Cameron moved away, sat up and put her feet on the floor. "I'm starving. We forgot to eat last night."

Sanjay laughed at her candor and threw the covers aside. "Yes, ma'am. Food first. I'll fix breakfast, and you get dressed."

"That's a gorgeous portrait in the guest room. Who is she?"

Sanjay rolled onto his side. His naked body positioned like the reclining Buddha in the recess above his bed. "My wife. We've been separated for several years."

Cameron reached for Sanjay's shirt and pulled it around her. She looked away. The word "wife" stung like fire.

"We got married in med school, both from traditional Indian families. She became quite western and decided she didn't want to stay in an arranged marriage. I didn't blame her."

"You never divorced?"

"She's taken a job in Miami. When she's settled, we'll finalize it."

"I see."

*

Before they finished breakfast, the gardener showed up at the back door. Sanjay kissed Cameron goodbye and he joined the other chain saw handlers in the neighborhood who had already begun removing trees and clearing their driveways. The sound of grinding wood and smell of burning fuel tinged the air. Cameron closed the door to the guest room. She didn't want those enormous black eyes watching her. His wife's eyes. Why did her portrait still hang here if they were getting divorced?

There was nothing to do but curl up on the sofa and watch the reports on TV. The hurricane had made landfall just north of Charleston, cutting a swath of destruction twenty miles wide and a hundred miles inland. Outlying islands suffered the most. Row upon row of waterfront mansions, many worth millions, had been sliced as if a giant sword cleaved them, dropping their walls into the raging sea, scattering furniture, rugs and clothing along the beach. Partially buried cars stuck out of the sand. Trees, mostly pines, stripped of their needles and doomed to die, fluttered with strips of rags.

At noon she heated soup Sanjay had left on the stove. Out the window she saw him coming toward the house. He walked into the garage and removed his dirty clothes before entering the kitchen door.

"A police car just pulled up at the end of the driveway," Cameron said. "Wonder if someone's trying to get in touch with you."

"I'll get dressed and go see. My father probably sent someone to check on me."

Before Sanjay reached the bedroom door, two police cruisers sped up the driveway, lights flashing. Four officers got out and ran toward the house.

The front door burst open. Dallas Rigsbee bounded into the room, his hand on his pistol. He looked from Cameron to Sanjay, an expression of contempt on his face.

"Why are you breaking into my home?" Sanjay demanded, stepping in front of Cameron.

"Cameron Patterson," the police chief boomed. "You're under arrest for the murder of Ernestine Gentry."

"What's happened to Ms. Ernie?" Cameron cried.

"You ought to know. You pushed her off the porch."

"Are you out of your mind, Dallas?"

Sanjay, dressed in nothing but his shorts, threw up his hands. "Wait a minute. There's been a mistake. Let me call my lawyer."

"Put your hands behind your back, Cameron," Dallas demanded.

"Let go of me," she cried and tried to pull away, but he wrenched her arms behind her back and snapped handcuffs on her wrists. "What's happened to Ms. Ernie?" she pleaded.

Dallas glanced around the room, targeting the box of marijuana on the coffee table. His eyes widened in surprise, and held it up for others to see. "Well, ain't this something?" He turned to face Sanjay. "Get your britches on, buster. Looks like you're going for a ride too."

Policemen that Cameron had never seen escorted her outside into a patrol car while Dallas read her rights. They shoved Sanjay into the other one. He called out to her. "Don't say anything. I'll call my lawyer when we get to the station."

A ride that should have taken thirty minutes took over an hour. People standing beside demolished houses ran out and flagged them down, begging for help. Other victims of the hurricane idly wandered along the side of the road, a look of disbelief on their faces. The response for help was the same for everyone. "Be patient. Someone will get to you soon as they can."

They passed crews of men repairing utility lines and clearing the roads. Children waded through roadside ditches, overflowing with filthy water that would soon breed swarms of mosquitoes. Cameron's pleas for information about

Ms. Ernie's death were met with silence from the two patrolmen. They'd been brought from Myrtle Beach to help Dallas and knew none of the details of the incident. Finally, she sat quietly, trying to imagine what could have happened. Ms. Ernie must have fallen off her porch. No one would have pushed her. But why would she, of all people, be accused of murdering that dear old lady?

Hobetown's jail, located in an antiquated building, would soon be replaced. Dallas Rigsbee boasted nightly at the cafe that he would have four new police officers when the new facility was completed. In the meantime, all lockups had to be taken to Clarendon, a town fifteen miles to the south.

Jimmy Markham looked up from the desk and turned away, embarrassed, when he saw Cameron—baggy pants and sloppy shirt, no bra.

"Jimmy," she said as they passed his desk. "Call Lynne. Tell her to get down here right now." Jimmy avoided her eyes but nodded his head.

"Looks like you're going to have to spend the night here with us," Dallas said. "Road to Clarendon's not open yet. Won't be able to find a magistrate today anyway."

Cameron balked. "You can't leave me here. It's filthy."

"Too bad, sweetheart. Can't have dangerous criminals like you roaming the streets. We'll get you out tomorrow."

The door clanged shut and Dallas walked

away. Cameron heard Sanjay's angry voice demanding to call his lawyer, then a cell door opened and closed, and footsteps sounded down the hall. After that, silence.

*

It wasn't long before Dallas unlocked Cameron's cell, and gripping her by the arm, led her down the hall to a windowless interrogation room. She heard the hum of a generator. To her relief, Jimmy Markham sat at the desk. She didn't want to be alone with Dallas.

Without making eye contact, Dallas motioned her to sit down.

"I need to call Danny Emerson," she said.

Dallas scratched his head, sparsely covered by thin wisps of hair, and wiped the perspiration from his forehead with a dirty handkerchief. He pulled at his crotch before settling his heavy bulk in a straight-backed chair.

"Lines are down. Besides, Danny drove his family to Atlanta."

"You can't keep me here."

"I can until your bail's set. No telling when that's going to be."

The smell of his body and cheap cologne repulsed her, and she turned away.

His eyes narrowed, angered by her look of contempt, and his face, already blotched and veined from too much alcohol, turned a hot red.

"You don't think I'd bring you in here just for the fun of it, do you?" He pushed away from the table and stood up, hiking his pants to the underside of his belly. Folds of fat hung over the collar of his shirt "I've got you cold, girl." He walked around the table, tugging at his belt, then returned to his chair and sat down.

Cameron leaned across the table. "Why are you doing this? You know I didn't kill Ms. Ernie."

"That's not what the eyewitness said."

"What eyewitness?"

"Good friend of yours, Short Cut Billy."

Cameron clapped her hands and burst out laughing. "You're crazier than I thought."

Dallas opened a file on the table. "William Henry Granger, aka Short Cut Billy, stated right here that he saw you push Ernestine Ray Gentry off her porch when she tried to stop you from taking a painting out of her house. He then saw you run across the street and enter your gallery carrying that painting. Later, you got into a big expensive car and drove away."

"That's absurd."

"When we got in touch with Buford he told us his mother had a valuable piece of art in her house. Got a warrant and found it hidden in your storage bin. How do you suppose it got there?"

The color drained from Cameron's face.

"Not so high and mighty now, are you, Cameron? Ready to sign a confession?"

"Go to hell, Dallas."

He took her arm and led her back down the hall to her cell, whistling softly. "By the way," he said, leaning down, his lips touching her ear. "Did I tell you how nice you look?"

*

At midnight, as Cameron huddled on the blanket Jimmy had brought to cover the fetid mattress, she looked up to see a tall, heavy-set man dressed in a business suit and carrying a briefcase, approaching her cell, his long strides making a hollow sound on the old wooden floor. He introduced himself as Hiram Kisker, attorney. He'd flown in from Atlanta after receiving a call from Dr. Rao. Jimmy fumbled to unlock the cell. The attorney shifted his weight impatiently.

"Sorry about all this, Cameron," Jimmy whispered in her ear, "I know you didn't kill Ms. Ernie."

"Where is Dr. Rao?" Cameron asked Hiram Kisker.

"At home, he's been released."

Easing Jimmy aside, the attorney took Cameron's arm and walked her down the hall through the outside door. "Dr. Rao posted your bail," he said. "I'll give you a ride home."

Cameron followed him. She had a dozen questions to ask, but she waited until they got in the car with her seat belt buckled. "The police chief said he has an eye witness who saw me push Ms. Ernie off her porch. That's impossible. I was with Dr. Rao all that time. We drove directly to his house after we left the gallery."

"Dr. Rao told me as much. Did you recognize anyone you passed on the road?"

"No. We saw a few pickups, a car or two."

"Anything memorable about any of them? Anything at all?"

Cameron could think of nothing. "Did they really find the painting in my gallery"

"Yes. The eyewitness claims he saw you carrying it across the street. Evidently Ms. Gentry had a masterpiece in her home."

"She had a copy of a Turner, just a copy."

"According to the police report, her son said that's what everyone was supposed to think, but it's the real thing."

"A genuine Turner in Hobetown?"

"When was the last time you saw the painting?"

"In her house when I stopped by before the hurricane. Billy, their eyewitness, was at the bottom of the steps. I tried to get him to go to a shelter, but he said he wanted to stay under the porch."

"Can you think of anyone who would have stolen it?"

"No."

"What about Billy?"

"He was drunk. Doubt if he could have

lifted it. He's the last person who would take it."

"Unless someone else wanted it and hired him."

She shook her head. "I don't think so."

"Who else has a key to the gallery?"

"Marsha, my assistant."

"That's all?"

"I think my friend Lynne has one. My daughter, too."

Hiram Kisker shifted in the seat. When he spoke again his voice was tight. "So, anyone could have the key."

"I guess so."

"You're positive the painting's a fake?" he pressed.

"What else could it be? Her father owned several copies of famous paintings."

"But you have no proof."

They turned on Short Street and Cameron pointed out her house. "You don't really think an authentic Turner could be hanging on a wall in Hobetown, do you?"

"That's not what I asked," was Hiram's quick reply. "Two years ago one turned up in a modest home in England. The heirs said it was a copy. Turned out to be authentic. It happens." Seeing the puzzled look on Cameron's face, he added, "I'm on the board at the High Museum. We keep up with that sort of thing."

He pulled into Cameron's driveway and left

the engine running. "You have a first appearance Wednesday morning at ten."

"Who'll be with me?"

"Do you have a local attorney?"

"Danny Emerson."

"I know the firm. I'll call him."

"I won't see you again?"

"Probably not. Mr. Emerson should be able to handle this." He got out and walked around the car to open Cameron's door. "I'll let Dr. Rao know you're home. I've advised him not to be seen with you in public. Small town gossip won't help you. There's also the professional ethics concern."

Cameron frowned, not sure what he meant.

"Rules apply to the amount of time that should pass before a relationship develops between a doctor and his former patient."

"What about me being at his house?"

"We can handle that. But for the time being, be discrete."

He surprised her by putting his hand on her shoulder and giving her a gentle squeeze. "The advice I give all my clients is try to relax and let us do our job. We're good at it. And don't talk about this to anyone unless you have a lawyer present. Not even your best friend."

LYNNE

The unfamiliar silence of the world outside awakened Lynne. She'd grown accustomed to the predawn avian concert announcing another day. What had happened to the birds? Had they found shelter? Would they return? She got out of bed and pulled the window curtain aside. The blood-red sun broke huge across the water. No cars passed, and no shouts from the men at the Fish House across the road who should be unloading the night's catch. The world seemed to have stopped. She put on the same clothes she'd worn the day before and walked outside. As far as she could see, broken tree limbs covered the ground. Neighbors who'd stayed through the storm were also out inspecting their property. Other than the hole in a roof, all the houses appeared to have escaped serious damage. She waved at the old man across the way. He waved back and gave her thumbs up.

Lynne removed the ladder, still propped against the well house door, and let out a sigh of relief. The paintings were unharmed. Later, she'd move them back to the studio.

She was hungry. She'd only eaten crackers and beer since yesterday. Nothing in the refrigerator was worth saving, but the freezer food hadn't thawed yet, so she packed her cooler with what she'd need for the next couple of days. She had just enough ice left to keep it cold until she got to town.

She could forget about Buddy showing up to help. Dallas had spoken the truth about that little weasel and the desk clerk. Everyone at the Ramada knew they were sleeping together. She might as well say goodbye to the five hundred dollars he owed her.

Her real concern was Dallas. He'd be back. He was the kind of creep who thought if he ever fucked you, he had a right to keep on doing it whenever it suited him. After she and Hubie had split, she'd had a fling with Dallas, a foolish waste of time on her part. But after months of suffering through Hubie's guilt, Dallas' bravado seemed refreshing. She'd dumped him by the time he and Cameron had their problem. There was a time when Dallas wasn't so bad, but too much alcohol and too many women, who left him for something better, had turned him into a nasty piece of trouble. She'd made an effort to stay below his radar. It was a good thing that he'd been preoccupied last night when he drove her home. The stink of male heat oozed from every pore, and if he'd decided to stay, she'd have been in real trouble.

Instead of feeling the pain of betrayal that usually sent her into a depression when the current guy walked out, she felt indifference. The thought of some randy, young stud rolling all over her and whispering dirty words to keep the action going, repulsed her, at least for now. She had more important things to do, but first she must exorcise the nagging guilt she'd felt since sleeping with Mark. As soon as she could find Cameron, she'd confess the whole stupid thing. Cameron would get mad, she had a right to, but hopefully, she'd forgive her. And with that off her conscience she'd get to work. Across a glass pane in the studio she wrote with Magic Marker, "Kick ass."

The rest of the morning she cleaned the studio, organized her brushes and paints, and sorted sketches, her mind fired with new ideas for paintings. At four o'clock the old man from across the street showed up and invited her to join a cookout. Neighbors were bringing the contents of their freezers to his house to grill. And they had ice to share.

*

The sun was barely up the next morning when she recognized the sound of Buddy's pickup rattling down the road. Still in her nightgown, she walked out on the porch and waited for him to get out of the truck. If he came looking for a little action, he was at the wrong place.

But from the look on his face she knew that wasn't what he wanted. Someone else must have died.

"Dallas arrested Cameron yesterday for Ms. Ernie's murder," he said.

Lynne stared at him, uncomprehendingly.

"Jimmy Markham came by looking for you. Woke me up. Said Short Cut Billy saw her throw Ms. Ernie off the porch. Some lawyer from Atlanta flew down in his private plane last night and got her out of jail."

"Where's she now?"

"Home, I guess. Nobody's seen her."

Monday, September 23

MICHAEL

Michael arrived at work early. He'd driven back to Hartford late Sunday after spending three nights at the shore. Most of the tourists were gone and he had the beach and restaurants to himself. He'd picked up a trashy novel and found a spot on the beach where he spent the weekend wondering why he didn't do that more often.

A note was waiting on his desk from Steff's father inviting Michael to join him for lunch in the executive dining room, a private restaurant on the top floor of their building where the town's legal barons gathered. People joked that more law was adjudicated in that room than in the courts. He'd only been invited to eat there once, when he was accepted into the firm. He wished he could talk with Stephanie before he met with her father. This was an awkward position to be in.

When his paralegal came by to welcome him back, he asked if their firm had an associate in Hobetown. Minutes later, she brought him a slip of paper with the name of Emerson and Emerson and a phone number. His call was switched to an answering service. Michael identified himself and said he sought information about Cameron Patterson. He was a friend and concerned about her.

He'd given up trying to reach Cameron. All weekend CNN ran footage of the devastation along the southern coast, including a quick shot of the damaged river front buildings in Hobetown. He wondered if anything was left of the cafe and its owner, Nell's old boyfriend.

The rest of the morning he spent going through files that had stacked up in his absence. Stephanie hadn't shown up for work. He asked the receptionist to let him know as soon as she came in.

At eleven-thirty he sat back and stared out the window at the tall buildings and hot streets alive with cars spilling toxic fumes. He thought of blue skies and clean mountain air, the heavy scent of pine, and Mahala Collins Weaver. She'd opened a part of him he didn't know existed. Money had never meant much to him, but he'd kept telling himself that this was what he'd worked so hard for. He looked around the office, a symbol of achievement only a week ago. Now he felt imprisoned.

He closed his eyes and pictured Big Mike and Haley resting beneath the pine tree while he'd continued on to the summit. The air at the top was cold and a light breeze swept through the falling leaves like the whisper of so many voices. He walked through the remains of a cabin and imagined that Big Mike's mother could have lived there. Beside the ruin, growing out of a patch of cleared ground, golden wildflowers turned their faces toward the sun. A sound caught his attention, and he looked down the path where a barefoot man, shotgun on his shoulder, was coming his way. Beneath his battered hat, hanks of brown hair hung around his shoulders. He had on overalls and no shirt. A Melungeon? Michael wanted to stop him so they could talk. They probably shared the same rogue gene. But the bearded man passed by without looking at Michael and disappeared down the trail. The apparition left him chilled, and he hurried down the mountain to rejoin Big Mike and Haley.

*

  Protocol demanded that he'd be waiting in the restaurant lobby for Wade Curtis to arrive, so he closed the file he'd been working on, straightened his tie and walked to the elevator. Stephanie's office door was still closed.
  Curtis was right behind him, in the next lift. "Sorry Maine didn't work out," he said, and gave Michael a friendly slap on the back. "Stephanie said you cancelled the fishing trip because of a family matter. Everything all right?"

"It will be."

"Glad to hear that. She was certainly disappointed, but she and her mother are having a good time in New York. I told them to stay another day. See a show. Make her mother happy."

They ordered lunch and Wade Curtis turned to Michael. "Stephanie tells me you have health issues. Of course I'm concerned. Is there something I could do to help?"

The salad arrived and Michael took a bite before he answered. He hadn't expected this.

"I guess you've heard that Steff and I had a misunderstanding."

"She said you were concerned about getting married until you have this health problem under control."

"Frankly, Mr. Curtis, it's more than my health. It's about commitment. Steff and I don't agree on what that means."

Wade Curtis placed his napkin on the table. "Stephanie said you'd gone south somewhere, looking for information about a genetic disease. Is that correct?"

"I might have an inherited disease called Familial Mediterranean Fever. I'm planning to start treatment right away."

"So, you should be okay?"

"I think so. I appreciate your concern and everything you've done for me. Working at this firm has been a great privilege." Michael paused and looked out the window at the skyscrapers.

"Do I detect ambivalence?" Wade Curtis asked.

"I guess so. I'd assumed Steff and I would get married and live happily ever after right here in this firm, but I'm not sure I'm the right person for her. I don't know if I can make her happy."

"Nonsense," Wade's voice boomed. "She's willful and spoiled, and I admit can be difficult as hell, just like her mother, but there's no question about her wanting to marry you. What else do you want?"

Mahala Weaver, Michael thought. "I guess I just want an uncomplicated relationship that I can depend on. Steff's a wonderful girl. I want what's best for both of us."

Wade Curtis took a deep breath, expanding his chest. He wore a hand tailored suit that Michael guessed cost four figures. The kind of suit he'd be wearing someday if he stayed with the firm.

"Marriage is the most important contract you'll ever sign," Wade said. "It's serious business and can either make or break you. I've seen men with brilliant career possibilities ruin everything because of a bad marriage. It's particularly important to a man who comes up the hard way, if you know what I mean."

Michael knew exactly what he meant.

"It's not enough to be smart."

Both men had ordered clam chowder, and when it arrived they ate in silence, looking up occasionally to nod at other lawyers having their lunch. No one approached the table, and Michael wondered if it was obvious this was a private matter.

"Dessert?" Wade asked, and looked at his watch.

"I'm fine."

"Then we better get back. I have an appointment in a few minutes."

They stepped off the elevator. Wade shook Michael's hand and suggested that they get together for dinner when Stephanie got back. Then he disappeared down the hall.

Michael's paralegal handed him a note from Daniel Emerson. He hurriedly read it. "Are you sure this is the right message?"

"Yes, sir," she answered. "I talked to Mr. Emerson personally. He said he's known Ms. Patterson all her life and would be representing her, along with Hiram Kisker in Atlanta. He suggested you talk directly to Mr. Kisker. He'd get back to you after he talked with Ms. Patterson."

Hiram Kisker! He was sure Cameron didn't know and couldn't afford that well-known criminal lawyer. Michael hurried down the hall to his office, then turned and came back. "Let me know when Mr. Curtis is free. I need to talk to him." The next words stuck in his throat. "And cancel my appointments for the rest of the week."

"All week?"

"Yes. I need to go to South Carolina."

*

When Michael explained that a family member had been arrested for murder, and Hiram Kisker represented her, Wade Curtis picked up the phone.

"You need to go down there. Let me give Kisker a call."

While he waited for the call to go through, he turned to Michael. "There's not a lawyer in the country that wouldn't jump at the chance to work with Kisker." He was too impressed with an opportunity to associate his firm with the legendary attorney to ask about Michael's relative.

Kisker took the call and told them that Dr. Sanjay Rao had hired him to represent Cameron Patterson. He felt the case was groundless and would be dismissed, but he was okay with Michael coming down, speeding things along. Despite the extra work Michael's absence would create, Wade Curtis was pleased.

On his way home Michael bought a hoagie at the corner deli to eat while he packed. He was on standby for the early morning plane to Atlanta. He'd be in Hobetown by three.

At nine o'clock, when he thought Haley would have Mindy in bed, he called. He pictured her in the silver house trailer sitting at her desk, blue jeans, tee shirt, long silky hair falling around her shoulders.

"I'm going to South Carolina tomorrow on business," he said. "Don't know how long it will take, but I could rent a car and drive out to see you on my way back."

Haley laughed. "Do you know how far that is? You might as well drive here from Connecticut."

"We could meet in Atlanta? Would you mind driving there?"

A pause. "Maybe."

"Tell me yes, Haley. I'll be staying at the Ritz Carlton."

"I might could come Thursday, but I'd have to leave Saturday. If I do I'll bring some stuff I found for you. You're gonna be surprised."

"Perfect. I'll get to the hotel about three. Counting on you being there," he said.

"If I'm not there by three, you know I'm not coming."

"If you're not there by three, I'm driving to Vardy to get you."

Haley burst out laughing. "What kind of a crazy man am I getting mixed up with"

"I'll see you Thursday. I'll let the hotel know you're coming. Don't disappoint me. The phones are down, but I'll try to call you from Hobetown."

"I can't believe I'm doing this."

At ten o'clock the buzzer rang. Stephanie was in the lobby. Michael stepped into the hall and waited for her to walk out of the elevator. She looked young and innocent in a white blouse and short denim skirt, her dark hair pulled back in a ponytail.

She brushed past him and sat on the sofa. "My father told me you're going to South Carolina tomorrow to help that woman. Why didn't you tell me?"

"I would have if I could have found you."

"Michael, why are you going down there?"

"Cameron Patterson has been falsely accused of murder."

"That's not your problem. You told my father she's a family member. You lied."

"I think of her as family. She's the only connection I have to my father."

"Bullshit."

"Steff, Cameron needs my help. That's all there is to it."

Stephanie took two beers out of the refrigerator. "I've been patient with you, but...."

"We need to talk," Michael said. "Sit down."

"Quit telling me what to do." She whirled around and pushed a beer into his chest. "Who the hell do you think you are? You'd be sitting on your ass in Boston if it wasn't for me."

He spoke calmly, the anger dissipated. "I'm sure it's my lack of sophistication, but I don't buy recreational sex. You obviously don't feel the same way."

"I've told you," Stephanie slammed her

hand on the coffee table, her face contorted in anger. "It had nothing to do with you."

"I don't want to argue. We see things differently. Let's be honest."

Stephanie settled back on the sofa, kicked off her sandals, and stretched out her long legs. "I made a mistake. It won't happen again." She patted the sofa cushion. "Come over here. Let's not talk about it anymore."

Michael didn't move.

Stephanie pressed her skirt down with the palms of her hands and leaned toward him. "We can agree to get over this and move on, or I'm going to walk out. I'm sorry I hurt you. Make up your mind." She tossed back her head and looked away. "Besides, my mother would be happy if I married someone else. Your pedigree leaves much to be desired."

It took all of Michael's resolve not to respond. He walked to the door and waited for her to stand up.

"I guess you're throwing me out." She walked slowly toward him, rolling her shoulders and swinging her hips. "Think I'll stay awhile. You're hot when you're angry." She put her arms around his neck and pressed her body against his.

It would be so easy to take her to bed and forget everything, but he pushed her back and looked into her eyes, softened with desire. "I can't handle you. I'm just a dumb son-of-a-bitch, but I know my limits."

Stephanie stiffened and dropped her arms. The fire returned to her narrowed eyes. "You really are a dumb son-of-a-bitch."

Tuesday, September 24

CAMERON

Cameron looked at the bowl of apples she'd sliced and was tempted to throw them out. Who would eat all this applesauce now that Nell was gone? Every fall she'd gathered these wormy pips from a neighbor's tree because Nell loved the tart, cinnamon-flavored sauce. She sprinkled them with lemon juice to keep from turning brown and covered the bowl with a towel. Cook it later.

Without a phone she'd been unable to talk to Sanjay. It had been two days since they'd been dragged into the police cars, and she needed to hear his voice. Danny was adamant about the two of them not being seen in public, and this sudden proscription left her filled with so much anxiety she couldn't sleep at night.

"It's just for a few days," Danny said. "You both have first appearances this week. Let's see how they go. I talk to Sanjay every day, and he says the same thing. 'Tell Cameron not to worry.

Everything's going to be all right.'" That was little comfort. She wanted to hear those words from him. Why couldn't he arrange to meet her in his office? He was her doctor. But second-guessing a man you barely knew and had fallen in love with was fool's play.

A car turned in the driveway. Probably Lynne, she thought. She dried her hands on her apron, tossed it over a chair and walked to the door.

Michael stepped out of the car. Before he reached the steps, Cameron flung open the door and ran out to meet him.

"I gave up trying to reach you." He hugged her. "Hope you don't mind if I just showed up. How are you doing?"

"Much better since I got out of jail." She locked her arm in his and walked toward the house then stopped, the smile gone. "I'm scared. I have a court date tomorrow afternoon."

"I know. That's why I'm here."

"Get your bag. You're staying here."

"What about Nell?"

Cameron's arms fell to her side. "She's disappeared, along with Callie, her birth mother. No one's seen them since the hurricane." She looked up at Michael and shook her head. "I don't know what to do."

Michael put his arm around her shoulder. "We'll find her."

He grabbed his suitcase from the car and

followed her into the house, up the creaking stairs to a second-floor bedroom.

"This was my room growing up," she said. "We rarely come up here anymore. Don't have much company." She opened a window. A damp breeze stirred the curtains. "It cools down at night."

Michael looked around the dormer room tucked under the roof. He laid his coat on the carved, four-poster bed, covered with a blue and white quilt, the same blue as in the wallpaper.

Cameron spread a luggage rack and put it at the foot of the bed, then pointed to a tall chest. "Put your things there." She opened a door to a closet that was cut in half by the slant of the roof.

"I'm on a generator. Only have electricity downstairs. The phones should be back on tomorrow." She considered a moment before she spoke and then said apologetically, "If you'd be more comfortable at the Ramada I understand, but I'd really like you to stay here."

"I'm fine here if you are." He removed his tie. "I understand that Dr. Rao's court appearance is this afternoon. I assume you're not going."

"Danny said not to."

"He's right. I can go for you."

MICHAEL

Michael climbed three flights of worn oak treads to the courtroom, stopping to admire the murals painted on the stairwell. Scenes above the wainscoting depicted Hobetown's better days: sailing ships docked along the river wharf, black men loading bales of cargo from mule-driven wagons, while women in bonnets and bright colored dresses accompanied by gentlemen in top hats and frock coats passed along the street smiling at one another. A feisty dog nipped at a little boy's heel.

Reporters lined either side of the room, poised with camera and notebook.

Michael took a seat in the back and looked around the gallery made up mostly of women whispering among themselves. Their eyes darted from door to door as they waited for the celebrity lawyer to appear.

The courtroom came alive the moment Hiram Kisker entered. Well over six feet, he carried himself with the confidence of a famous man. He and Dr. Rao took their seats. An attractive woman whom Michael thought looked Indian, perhaps the doctor's relative, sat behind them in the first row. Flash bulbs exploded and spectators craned their necks to get a better look. Gathered at the opposite table, the district attorney's team stared across the aisle. Before the bailiff called out "all rise," Hiram Kisker was on his feet. The judge entered, a scowl on his face, and looked over the courtroom.

Behind Michael the door swung open and an elderly gentleman dressed in an embroidered caftan walked into the courtroom, his head wrapped in a turban, a cabochon ruby as large as a bird's egg pinned to the headdress. Flanking him, two men in business suits carrying slim briefcases walked erect as color guards directly up to the judge. A buzz went up in the courtroom, and the judge pounded his gavel demanding quiet. He accepted the intruder's credentials, examined them thoroughly, and looked from one to the other as he read the papers they presented. The district attorney bolted to his feet demanding to know what had happened, but the judge motioned him to sit down while he read and reread the documents. Hiram Kisker stared at the bench, his expression incredulous, his mouth tightened to a slash. Dr. Rao slumped in his chair. The Indian-looking woman sitting behind him reached forward and patted his shoulder.

Muttering to himself, the judge pushed the papers aside and fixed his gaze on Bandar Rao. "The gentleman before me is Bandar Rao, cultural attaché and member of the diplomatic corps attached to the Indian Embassy in Washington. As such he has diplomatic immunity. He is the owner of the substance allegedly identified as marijuana found in the home of his son, Dr. Sanjay Rao. We have a letter from Bandar Rao's physician in Delhi stating that this substance is a medical remedy, prescribed for him and essential to his well being." He paused and looked at the stunned district attorney. "I see no other course than to dismiss this case."

The DA jettisoned to his feet and asked for a continuance, but the briefcases stepped forward and the judge threw up his hands.

"Case dismissed," he growled, and pounded the gavel. It took several seconds before the media understood what had happened, and they clamored to reach Hiram Kisker, but he ducked his head and charged toward the stairs repeating "No comment, no comment."

Michael decided that this was not the time to introduce himself to the lawyer. He backed off and watched the entourage exit the room. The Indian woman walked beside Dr. Rao's father who nodded and smiled to the reporters as he passed.

DALLAS RIGSBEE

A young man looking enough like Sy Patterson to be his twin diverted the police chief's attention from the drama in the courtroom. After the surprise dismissal, Dallas watched him approach the big-shot lawyer, hesitate, then turn and hightail it out of the courtroom. He followed him down the steps and watched as he made a beeline toward the river.

Dallas would liked to have stayed in the court room because the lawyer from Atlanta looked pissed, like he might blow up any minute, and he hated to miss the show, but he had a bad feeling about the outsider.

Dallas got in his car and eased down the street. A hundred yards ahead of the stranger he stopped and waited. When the man walked by, Dallas rolled down the window. "You looking for somebody?"

"Just getting my car."

"I seen you in the courtroom."

"That's right."

Dallas waited for an explanation. This wasn't the normal reaction for someone talking to the police chief. Most people blabbed on and on about where they'd been and what they'd been up to, giving all kinds of stupid details, as if anyone gave a damn, but this young fellow in his city clothes stood quietly, looking him in the eye and waiting.

"New in town?" Dallas asked.

"I've been here before. Too bad it's so torn up."

"What'd you say your name was?"

"Michael Duncan. Is there a problem?"

"You tell me." Dallas rolled down the driver's side window and spat a stream of tobacco juice onto the street. "On your way out of town?"

"Not yet," Michael replied. He returned to the sidewalk and without looking back, continued down the street.

Dallas watched the stranger until he reached his car in the cafe lot then made a U-turn and followed him to Short Street.

MICHAEL

Michael walked into the kitchen and sniffed the mouthwatering aroma of baked chicken. His stomach growled in anticipation. He was hungry and tired. Cameron looked up and smiled. When he'd arrived she'd been wearing shorts and a sleeveless shirt. Now, she'd changed into a pair of white pants and a silk blouse, the same blue as her eyes. She'd pulled her blonde hair back into a clip, her eyes, outlined in mascara, looked large and luminous. He liked that she'd done this for him, but he knew enough about women not to draw too much attention to that effort, so he just told her how nice she looked. "Smells good in here," he said.

"The least I can do is feed you. Hope you like turnip greens. My neighbor dropped off a batch."

"I like anything you cook." He pulled out a chair.

"Tea or beer?"

"I need something cold. I'll have a beer."

Cameron laughed. "When southerners say tea, they mean iced tea. I forgot I was talking to a

Yankee."

"I'm learning." Watching her move around the kitchen, Michael couldn't understand how a woman as attractive as Cameron would remain a widow for seven years. When he got to know her better, he'd ask.

Cameron listened to his description of the courtroom scene, laughing with surprise and amusement as Michael described how exasperated the wizened old curmudgeon, Judge Wilcox, was to have had such antics take place in his courtroom.

"An attractive woman sat behind Dr. Rao. Looked like a relative."

Cameron put the plates down on the table and stood motionless for several seconds. "I think I know who that is," she finally said.

"What's wrong?" Michael asked.

"That's his wife. They've been separated for years, but she's obviously come back."

"He didn't tell you?"

"I haven't talked to him."

Michael didn't know what to say. If that guy's wife was back, he should have let Cameron know. Not keep her wondering.

*

After dinner dishes were put away, Cameron walked out to the back porch and called to Michael. "Come have a seat. It's cooler here."

Threads of red and gold streaked across the sky as the fading sun gathered its remaining light and dropped behind the horizon. Michael pulled a rocker close to her. She put her finger to her lips. "Hush," she whispered. "You're about to hear the twilight song."

He wasn't sure what to expect, but he sat back and rocked, thinking that one of the many churches he'd passed rang their bells this time of day. That's the kind of thing he'd expect in a place like Hobetown. But minutes later a chorus of birds sang out so loudly that he sat up with a start.

"What is it?" he asked.

"Birds. They sing like that at dawn and dusk."

They listened to the song that lasted a full minute before it stopped as suddenly as it began. Michael turned to Cameron. "I've never heard anything like that."

"That's what happens when you grow up in a city."

"I'm beginning to change my mind about Hobetown. It grows on you."

"Your father loved this town. You will too if you stay around."

"Wish I could, but I've got to get back to Hartford. Personal stuff."

"Bet there's a woman in there someplace."

"Is it that obvious?"

"At your age, what else? You mentioned

you had a fiancée."

"I've met another woman."

Cameron let out a sigh. "Oh dear. Better now than later."

"You sound like my grandfather."

"The need to find someone, the right one, never leaves you. You can push it aside, find substitutes, but it's always there. You're lucky if you find that person early."

"Were you and my father happy together?"

"Very."

"Can you be happy with someone else?"

"I hope so."

They fell silent. Michael's thoughts turned to Haley and Atlanta. He hoped she'd be there waiting for him Thursday. He'd take her to the history museum. She'd love that. Then to the High if they had enough time. He glanced at Cameron. She sat silent, her expression impossible to read. He guessed that her mind was full of tomorrow's court appearance. She didn't express her concerns, or ask about his. Michael liked that about her. They could sit quietly without the need for conversation. Maybe it was a southern thing. Haley was the same way. He was accustomed to women like his mother and Steff who hated silence.

Wednesday, September 25

MICHAEL

Hubie Odum stopped by early the next morning to bring Cameron gas for her generator. When he met Michael coming down the steps he dropped the can and stared, mouth agape, muttering, "Well goddamn, goddamn."

Michael didn't mind people knowing he was a Patterson as long as Cameron was okay with it, but this reaction had gotten old. Her friend Lynne came by the night before and burst into tears when she saw him.

He wanted to check out the crime scene before Cameron's two-thirty court appearance, so he left Hubie and Cameron standing in the yard and set out on foot, picking his way down the littered street toward River Road. It hadn't taken long to realize that walking was the easiest way to get around town.

Most of the damage in Cameron's neighborhood confined itself to torn shutters and missing shingles. Two houses he passed, struck by fallen trees, sported bright blue tarps that rippled and flapped against the exposed holes. Neighbors were out raking their yards, piling debris along the street, and they waved as he passed. He returned their friendly gestures and walked on, wondering if they thought they'd seen a ghost.

As Michael got closer to the river the devastation increased. Electrical lines dangled from broken poles. The scraping sound of front loaders and their monotonous beep, beep, beep, echoed at every corner as they pushed and loaded mangled trees onto dump trucks.

He'd packed his camera in his backpack. Big Mike would be interested in seeing what a hurricane could do to a small town. After he took pictures of the waterfront buildings he planned to walk to Sunrise Avenue.

As he approached the cafe, Michael recognized the owner dragging a soaked carpet across the parking lot.

"How you doing?" Steve called out and wiped his hand on the back of his pants before extending it to Michael. "Steve McLean. You're the Patterson relative aren't you? How are things going? I mean with Cameron. Heard you came down to help."

"She has a good lawyer."

"What about Nell?"

"Cameron hasn't seen her since the hurricane."

Steve shook his head. "I was afraid of that. She and Callie?"

"You know Callie?"

"Half the town knows her. She practically lived in the bar."

Steve tugged at the carpet. Michael grabbed the other end and helped him throw it on the pile of trash.

"They came in here the first night Callie got to town. Nell was excited about showing off her real mother. Pathetic." Steve grimaced. "Callie's a drunk. Wouldn't leave the bar. Nell said she couldn't take her back to her grandmother's house in that condition so she checked into the Ramada. Same thing the next night."

"Where do you think they've gone?" Michael asked.

"Don't know, but I can tell you that something's not right. I overheard her and Callie talking about money that Nell's supposed to get, ten thousand dollars. I came right out and asked her where she'd get that kind of money."

"What did she say?"

"Told me to mind my own business." He dug his hands in his pockets and stared down at his feet. "Hope she's not in trouble. Nell's a good girl, a little crazy at times. Her being adopted and all that, and Sy dying."

"Mind if I mention this to Cameron?"

"No, that's why I'm telling you. They'll

dismiss the charges against Cameron, won't they? Everyone knows she didn't push Ms. Ernie off the porch."

"They ought to." Michael pulled out the camera. "Thought I'd take some pictures. We've never seen anything like this where I come from."

"Be careful where you step." Steve pointed toward the end of the parking lot. "Stand over there. You get a good view of what's left of the buildings. River just ate 'em up."

Yellow tape to prevent looting roped off the battered boardwalk. Buildings, their backs ripped off, hung over the river. It reminded Michael of a giant dollhouse. In the upper apartments, tables and chairs lay scattered and broken, and plumbing fixtures, stubbornly connected to the pipes, dangled in the air. Clothing, caught on splintered pieces of wood, fluttered in the soft breeze. It struck Michael that taking pictures of these people's hard luck was an insensitive invasion of privacy, and he put the camera in his backpack. He answered the quizzical look on Steve's face. "Changed my mind. I wouldn't want people taking pictures of my disaster, would you?"

"See what you mean," Steve replied.

"Catch you later," Michael said and continued his walk to Sunrise Avenue, his mind stuck on that ten thousand dollars Nell expected to get. He and Cameron needed to talk.

In the distance he saw the yellow crime tape

spread around both the gallery and Ms. Gentry's home. As he approached, a car drove up. The woman he recognized as Ms Ernie's helper got out, ducked beneath the tape and climbed the stairs to the upper apartment. Moments later Short Cut Billy appeared from behind the house.

Michael, hands in his pockets and nonchalantly kicking bits of rubble from his path, walked up to Billy. "Sure is a mess around here."

"She was a big 'un all right. Near 'bout blew me away."

"I understand the lady who lived in this house died during the storm," Michael said.

"Terrible thing." Billy shook his head, sadly. "Ms. Ernie fell off that porch and broke her neck. Seen the whole thing."

"You say she fell off the porch?" Michael walked as close to the house as the yellow tape would permit and looked up at the hole where the rotten railing, still lying on the ground, had been.

"Ain't rightly sure what happened so much going on that morning," Billy stammered.

The upstairs door opened and the woman walked out on the porch and down the steps, carrying a garment bag. She cast a sullen glance at Billy who tipped his head and backed away.

"Getting Ms. Ernie some burial clothes?" he asked.

"Yes, and don't you go talking about it. You've already said too much."

Billy stared over Michael's shoulder at the approaching police cruiser.

"What ya'll doing down here?" a voice called out. Michael recognized the police chief's drawl.

Billy hopped from one foot to the other, rubbing his hands and shaking his head. "Nothing, Chief."

"You're not supposed to be down here. Neither of you."

"Checking out the gallery," Michael said.

"That's our job. Unless you got a court order, you can't trespass beyond the tape."

Michael nodded.

"Billy, get in the car," the chief ordered.

The wobbly derelict ducked his head and pulled in his frail shoulders. Michael thought he looked frightened, but Billy obediently walked around the car and got in the back seat.

"Through with your business in town?" the Chief asked.

"Just about," Michael replied.

On his walk back to Cameron's, Michael stopped at the courthouse. He righted the bench beneath a battered tree, then sat down and looked toward the river below. The sky, scrubbed clean by the powerful winds, was a blue he'd never seen. Hobetown was definitely growing on him. Even its nosey townspeople. What would it be like to own a little place down here? One of these musty old houses where he'd throw open the doors and windows and walk around barefoot, hot and sweaty. Big Mike would like that. They'd get a boat and fishing gear and stay on the water as long as they wanted. And when they'd had enough they'd sit on the porch and listen to the birds sing, and watch the sunset. Although it was a dream, it had enough possibility to get him excited.

*

When Michael returned to Short Street he found Cameron dressed in a navy blue cotton suit and white blouse talking with Danny Emerson.

"Mr. Kisker said you'd be stopping by." Danny shook Michael's hand. "Appreciate your being here." He looked at Cameron. "So does she. I've been explaining that they don't have much of a case. We'll get it dismissed."

"No case at all, as I can see. I ran into Short Cut Billy a little while ago. He told me he saw Ms. Ernie fall off her porch."

Danny cocked his head. "What Billy tells you and what he told Dallas are two different things. They have a sworn statement that he saw Cameron push her."

"We'll get him on the stand," Michael said.

"Will he be in court today?" Cameron asked.

"If not, they don't have a case," Michael replied.

"It's not a slam dunk," Danny warned. "Dallas has it in for Cameron, and we all know that he's a mean s.o.b. with too much power."

* * *

Only a handful of townspeople showed up for Cameron's appearance, along with two reporters. The DA paced the center aisle looking at his watch and eying the door. Judge Wilcox entered the room, his head down, like a charging bull, and the DA returned to the table.

"Will the defendant rise?"

Cameron got to her feet.

"How do you plead to charges of murder?"

"Not guilty, your honor."

Dallas entered the courtroom, panting from his climb to the third floor and wiped his dripping brow. He whispered in the DA's ear.

"Would you like to share that with us?" the judge quipped.

The DA stepped forward. "The chief of police has informed me that our witness, William Granger, is nowhere to be found."

Judge Wilcox, red-faced and angry, looked at Dallas. "Is that true?"

"I don't know where the little son-of-a-bitch is. I had him earlier this morning."

Danny Emerson exchanged looks with Michael then approached the bench. "Your honor, I request that the charges be dismissed."

"We have an eyewitness," spoke up the DA. "We will produce him."

"When do you think that might be?" asked the judge, pushing back from his desk.

"I'll find him," Dallas said.

The judge gathered his papers. "I'm not ready to dismiss this case just yet. I'll reset this hearing for one week from today. And Mr. Cox, you better have your witness here."

An elderly woman wearing a dark dress and straw hat stopped Cameron on her way out of the courtroom. She put her arms around her, enfolding her in a strong hug. "Everyone knows you didn't do this," the woman said. "People are praying for you all over town."

"Thank you, Ms. Eubanks."

"A whole lot of folks wanted to come today, but we passed the word around to stay home. Ms. Ernie's death had nothing to do with you. I say let the poor woman rest in peace."

Michael told Cameron to ride back to the house with Danny. He had a stop to make. He'd join them later, and they'd have dinner together. He wanted to surprise Cameron with a bottle of champagne, even if a celebration was premature. He wouldn't be around when the case was dismissed.

Cameron was waiting for him, waving a piece of paper. "Thelma left a note. Nell's at the Starlight Motel in downtown Atlanta."

"I'm going up there in the morning. I'll go by," Michael said.

Cameron's smile faded. "So soon?"

"I'll be back." Michael handed her the champagne. "This is to celebrate today's victory."

Cameron took the bottle. "We'll save it 'til you come back."

*

Because most the restaurants within driving distance were closed for repairs, Cameron had a pot of shrimp Creole and a skillet of cracklin' cornbread ready to put in the oven.

"I'm going to hold you to our celebration dinner," she said in response to Michael's apology for not being able to take her out.

"You do that. But I don't care where we go, it won't be as good as your cooking."

After dinner they carried their coffee to the porch. There was so much Michael needed to talk to Cameron about, but he was running out of time. He wanted to think that he'd come back, but that wasn't likely. Too many decisions about his life had to be made and none of them included Hobetown.

"Ran into Steve today," he said. "He overheard Nell and Callie talking about ten thousand dollars Nell is supposed to get. Know anything about that?"

"She and Callie wanted to start a business. Nell told me she had an investor. I didn't believe it, but now I think I know who it is."

"Does it have anything to do with the painting?" Michael said.

"I think Buford, Ms. Ernie's son, hired Nell to steal the painting. Buford believes it's a genuine Turner."

"Why would he steal his mother's painting? Wouldn't it be his eventually?"

"Maybe she planned to leave it to someone else. I'm sure I interrupted a conversation between Nell and Buford that day you were here. The reason I remember it so vividly is because Nell barely speaks to Buford. When I walked in she looked like I'd caught her doing something wrong. I know the look."

"Have you told Danny Emerson this?"

"No, even if Nell took it, she wouldn't hurt Ms. Ernie. I'd stake my life on that."

"We need to find Nell and clear this up."

Thursday, September 26

MICHAEL

Michael entered Hiram Kisker's thirtieth-floor empire to find the lawyer seated at his desk, silhouetted against the bright light that streamed through a wall of windows behind him. The effect was intimidating, but the greeting was friendly. "Emerson said you were a big help to Cameron."

"I didn't do much, but I was glad to be there," Michael responded. "I wished I could have stayed longer."

"You can always go back. I'm sure you'd be welcome." Hiram's words weren't lost on Michael. Danny Emerson had no doubt told him of his relationship to Cameron.

"I might just do that. I'm making a change in my life and…" Michael stopped, embarrassed he blurted out personal information that had nothing to do with this meeting. He recovered and took a seat.

Hiram pointed to a packet of papers on his

desk. "Ms. Gentry's will. She set up a trust for the sale of the painting with Cameron Patterson as trustee. Cameron is instructed to use the funds to refurbish a warehouse Ms. Gentry owned. Wants it turned into a homeless shelter. The rest of her property is left to her son Buford."

"It would be to his advantage to get it away from her as soon as possible, wouldn't it?" Michael asked.

"My thoughts entirely," Hiram responded.

"Cameron thinks Buford paid her daughter to steal it. She disappeared right after the storm. Turned up in a motel here in Atlanta."

"That's an interesting piece of the puzzle. Sounds like it fits." Hiram drummed his fingers on the desk before he spoke. "I'd like to get Buford's side of the story. Do you think he'll talk to you?"

"I can try."

"If Cameron's right, Buford could straighten this whole mess out. See what you can learn. Let's get this case dismissed before we have to go back to court."

"Where' the painting?" Michael asked.

"It's been sent to the High Museum for appraisal. I'm expecting a call from the curator any time."

"Is it possible that a genuine Turner could have hung on that wall all these years and no one knew?" Michael asked.

"Stranger things have happened, but we'll know soon enough."

At the door the two men shook hands. "How about eleven, tomorrow?" Hiram handed Michael a card. "If you need to get in touch with me before then, here's my number."

Michael stopped in the conference room to check his home phone for messages. There was nothing from Haley, which was good news. He hoped she was on her way. He made a note of Buford's home address in the phone book. He'd pay him a surprise visit after he tracked down Nell.

It didn't take long to find The Starlight Motel, a cinderblock building, squatting in a jungle of boarded-up stores and overflowing dumpsters, not far from the entrance to Underground Atlanta.

The owners had made few concessions to luxury, but what they did offer was immediate proximity to the restored, centuries-old city below the modern streets, famous for its clubs and nightlife. Michael spotted a Crown Victoria with Florida plates in front of room 32—curtains drawn, and a "Do Not Disturb" sign hanging from the corroded knob. He rapped on the door.

"Who is it?" a groggy voice responded.

"Michael Duncan. Open up."

He heard shuffling sounds and high-pitched voices bantering back and forth before the door opened and Nell stood before him, one eye smudged with the stain of last night's mascara. Behind her, he glimpsed another woman pulling on blue jeans.

"What are you doing here?"

"Your mother's worried about you. You should let her know where you are."

"I'm fine. Quit bothering me." Nell tossed her head in Callie's direction. "Besides, my mother's here." She started to close the door but Michael eased his shoulder forward.

"We need to talk."

Nell looked around the room. "It's a mess in here. Let's go across the street to the diner. Get some coffee."

"Late night?" Michael asked, when they'd settled in a booth in front of the window.

"Very. Callie thinks she has to close every bar in town."

Nell ordered two hamburgers, one to go. Michael held up the stainless steel napkin dispenser in front of her face. "Take a look. Makeup's running down your face."

"What do you expect? Wake me up and drag me out." She began furiously scrubbing at her face with a napkin. "Quit looking at me like that," she snapped.

"That's better." He took the holder from her hand. "I want you to tell me about the painting."

"What are you talking about?"

"You know what I'm talking about. The painting you took from Ms. Ernie's house."

Nell's head dropped and she began to sob.

"I know Buford put you up to it."

"I didn't kill the old lady. Cameron didn't either. She fell off the porch."

"That's not what the police think."

"It's the truth. I was all the way across the street when I heard her yelling at me, and the porch rail cracked. I didn't know she was in there."

"You had the painting?"

"Buford said she'd give it to that bunch of drunks she feeds if he didn't get it out of there. He said I wasn't stealing anything because it was rightfully his, and he didn't want to have to go to court to get it away from her."

"So he paid you to get it?"

"She wasn't supposed to be there. Said he'd arranged for her to go to the Ramada. She must have been back in her bedroom. When I heard her hit the ground I put the painting down and ran back as fast as I could, but her head was at a horrible angle. I knew she was dead." Nell buried her head in her hands, tears streaming down her face.

"What did you do with the painting?"

"As soon as I got it inside the gallery, I was supposed to call Buford at a number he gave me. He said he'd be waiting someplace in town and would drive by and get it."

"Then what happened?"

"I called him and said I thought his mother was dead. He was raving, crazy mad and told me to put the painting in my car and bring it to him, but I didn't have a car. I walked there. So he said to hide it in a storage bin in the gallery, and he'd get it later. I saw Billy crawl out from under the steps and pull Ms. Ernie on the porch, then run for help. I told Buford, and he said to get out of there as fast as I could and say nothing to no one."

"When did you talk to Buford again?"

"Later that day. Callie and I drove up here ahead of the storm. Nearly got blown off the road. Checked into the motel and called him. All he'd say was that he'd be in touch. I knew he was going to stiff me. Callie said we needed to stay in Atlanta and make him pay up."

"Why haven't you told someone?"

"I did. I called Dallas. Told him what happened. He just laughed at me. Said I was lying to save my mother, but it wasn't going to work. He had an eyewitness."

"Did you tell Buford this?"

"He told me to keep my mouth shut. Anything I said would only make matters worse. Said the charges were going to be dropped and the whole thing would go away. If I said one word about it, he wasn't going to give me the money."

"What did he offer you?"

"Five thousand dollars when he picked it up and another five after it sold. Callie and I planned to use that to open a cleaning business." Nell wiped her eyes on her sleeve. "He hasn't given me anything."

"Have you talked to him since?"

"Yesterday. I waited outside his building.

Told him that if he didn't call Danny Emerson and tell him the truth, I would. He said go ahead. He'd swear I lied. Why would he steal his own painting? We'd see who the judge believed. I don't know what to do."

"I think you do, Nell."

Nell slumped in the booth and started crying again. "Callie's driving me crazy. Wish I'd never met her. All she talks about is getting the money. She doesn't care if Cameron goes to jail."

"Do you?"

Nell's face twisted in anger and she fired back, "Of course I do."

"Go home and let her know you're all right. Steve's worried about you too."

"Really?" Her eyes brightened, and she almost smiled. "He tried to warn me about Callie, but I didn't want to listen."

"I understand what you've been going through, Nell, but you know who your real mother is. Call her. Steve, too. The phones are working."

The diner door opened and Callie entered, looked around and walked over to the table. "I thought I'd find you here. What y'all up to? What you crying about, Nell?" She looked from one to the other and pulled a sad face. "I want to tell ya'll right now that I don't know nothing about none of this."

"Call your mother," Michael said, ignoring Callie. "I'm staying at the Ritz Carlton for a couple of days. You can reach me there." He stood up and tossed money on the table. "I'll be waiting to hear from you."

*

The desk clerk told Michael that his guest had arrived and handed him two messages. Stephanie had called. He hadn't expected that. The other was from Big Mike wanting to know when he'd be home. He had good news. Michael smiled to himself. The good news was probably that his mother had finally decided to marry that guy who'd been hanging around. Thank God. Life would be much simpler for all of them.

On the way to the room, he removed his tie and put it in his pocket, then took a quick look at himself in the smoked elevator mirror. He should have told the desk clerk to hold his calls. He didn't want any more interruptions.

He found Haley curled up in an oversized chair that swallowed her tiny frame. She had on a yellow sundress, gold hoop earrings and a strand of pearls. He'd heard Steff refer sarcastically to "those strand-of-pearls" girls who worked in the office. He was never quite sure why that was a derisive comment, but he liked the way they looked on Haley. Her hair, loosely braided in a single plait, hung down her back.

"Just resting my eyes," she said and smiled.

"Sorry to be late."

"It's all right. Gave me a chance to look

around."

"Like what you see?"

"Sure do, fine place. Even has a workout room in the basement where you can get a massage and facial."

"We'll have to treat you to that."

Haley laughed and stood up. "Not a good idea, I might get used to it."

"You're more beautiful than I remember," Michael said, in spite of himself.

Haley looked away.

Michael knew to be cautious with her. Go slow and let her set the pace. He looked at his watch. "What do you say we go downstairs and have a drink?"

Haley nodded, took a quick peek at herself in the mirror and followed him out the door.

He ordered martinis for them after Haley said she'd never had a real one.

"Umm," she purred after the first sip. "This is good."

"But lethal, so take your time. Our reservation is not for a couple of hours."

"I'm not much of a fancy drinker," she said. "Not much of a drinker period."

Her simple straightforward manner was so endearing he wanted to hug her. Instead, he smiled and asked her to tell him about the Patterson research she'd gathered for him.

"I searched court records, birth, death and marriage certificates and wills. The Pattersons came into North Carolina in the early eighteen hundreds. Had lots of land and lots of younguns. One of them also had an illegitimate son by an Indian woman. His name was Sylvester. He's listed as a mulatto in the 1890 census."

"That might explain the Indian grandmother legend. The family claims that one of their great-grandmothers was Indian," he said.

"She must have been something special because Sylvester had his father's surname. If he was illegitimate, he should have had his mother's."

"Maybe they were married."

"Interracial marriages were illegal."

"But she was Indian, not black."

"Same thing back then. Anyway, Sylvester eventually passed for white because he moved to the next county and married a prosperous white woman. There's no more mention of mulatto after that."

"Does this tie into the Melungeons?"

"Yes indeed. The Melungeons moved into central North Carolina a hundred years before the Pattersons and intermarried with a tribe of interracial Indians. If you ask me, that grandma is one of those Indians, and that's where the gene came from."

"Sy Patterson and my mom met and bingo! Those genes got connected again."

"And here you are." Haley laughed. "You and I better be thinking about who we have children with. You don't want to be passing on bad genes."

"It's a little late for that," Michael said.

Haley made no comment and Michael wondered if she was thinking about her little girl, or children she might have in the future.

"I don't know how to thank you, Haley. Feels like I'm discovering a part of me that's been buried."

"There's something magical about finding folks who lived a long time ago. Specially when you're related to them. Kinda like looking in a broken mirror."

"Like seeing different images of yourself?"

"Something like that. Does it bother you knowing one of your ancestors was a mulatto?"

"Not at all. I'm just glad to know the truth. Bet old Sylvester never thought his descendants would be talking about him a hundred years later, discovering his secrets."

Haley looked up at Michael, her face softened with admiration. "Bet he'd have liked it."

At seven-thirty, Michael said it was time to go to a nearby restaurant where he'd made reservations, but Haley wanted to stay at the Ritz Carlton and eat in their dining room. She said she didn't need any place nicer. Besides, she felt a little shaky. She wasn't accustomed to martinis, although she could see why people made such a fuss about them.

Over a candlelit table sparkling with silver

and crystal, Haley asked Michael to choose from the menu.

He ordered a bottle of wine, but after one sip she pushed the glass away. "I don't need any more. Tell the waiter to bring the cork, and we'll take it."

"We don't need to do that."

"Shame to waste it." She put her hand to her head. "I'm spinning like a top. I better go up to the room."

On the ride up the elevator Haley leaned against Michael, humming, her eyes closed. He hadn't intended for this to happen—wanted a wide-awake and responsive Haley—but he helped her in the room and steered her toward the bed.

"Okay if I help you undress?" he asked.

She weaved, trying to steady herself, then fell back against the cover. "I'm so ashamed," she whispered.

"Don't be, it's my fault. I didn't mean for you to drink too much. Rest a little, and you'll feel better when you wake up."

He slipped off her sandals and unzipped her dress. Underneath she wore nothing but a lacy strapless bra and panties. He covered her with the blanket, and in seconds she'd fallen asleep.

For the next couple of hours, he lay next to her and watched television. She barely moved. At eleven o'clock he got undressed, turned off the TV and crawled under the covers. She rolled over, made a soft sound and put her arm across his chest. Carefully, Michael drew her to him, resting her head on his shoulder.

During the night he awoke to the sound of water running. The bathroom door opened and Haley walked into the room wrapped in a towel.

Michael sat up in bed. "You all right?"

"Just embarrassed," she sighed. "Bet you're sorry you ever laid eyes on me."

"No way, Haley. Sorry you don't feel well."

"Would you mind getting me my robe?"

Michael opened her suitcase and removed a silky, pale robe wrapped in tissue paper, the way it had come from the store. He unfolded it and took it to her. She slipped her arms in the sleeves and dropped the towel, then stood a moment, uncertain what to do, before Michael led her to the bed.

"It's okay," he said. "You're in charge." He hugged her to him. "Would you like something from room service?"

"I don't think so." She slipped under the blanket and rolled on her side, watching him. "You might be the nicest man I've ever met."

Michael got in bed beside her and drew her to him. "You just might be the nicest woman I've ever met." He kissed her forehead. She moved closer and the robe slipped from her shoulder. He kissed her lips that were eager to respond. Her small breasts pressed against him and he ran his hands down her back.

"I think it's time for you to be in charge," she said and threw her arms around him.

CAMERON

Cameron had gotten up early to make Michael breakfast. He'd said not to bother, he'd stop on the drive to Atlanta, but she couldn't help herself. She had to see him off. The sound of the telephone ringing startled her, and she turned the fire off under the scrambled eggs and answered it.

"Finally." Danny Emerson was on the line. "We got the phones back last night. Is Michael still there?"

"Hang on a minute."

Michael came down the steps, and she handed him the phone. After a short conversation he hung up and turned to her. "I wouldn't worry about it, but Danny wanted me to know that Dallas is pressuring the DA not to drop the charges against you. He'll call you after he talks to Dallas."

"And I'm not supposed to worry?"

Michael held her face in his hand. "I promise you it will be okay. Dallas is posturing. There's no case here."

After breakfast she walked with him to the car.

"I'll stay in touch, Cameron," he said. "If I don't call you tonight, don't worry. It's because I don't know anything, but I'll definitely call tomorrow." He put his arms around her and held her a long time before he gently pushed her away.

"Promise you'll come back," she said.

"I owe you that dinner. I've got to come back."

She watched him pull out of the driveway and head down Short Street, then turned and went back inside.

By ten o'clock she'd cleaned his room and laundered the sheets. The house echoed with emptiness. She'd never felt so alone, but then she'd never been alone in this house. If this is how life was going to be, she needed to know, and she picked up the phone and called Sanjay's office.

She left a message with the answering service to call her and she sat down to wait. Fifteen minutes later he called. His voice was warm but guarded. Was she okay? He was sorry he hadn't been able to see her. Would she be home later? They needed to talk, but now wasn't convenient. He'd call back.

She hung up the phone and burst into tears. It wasn't convenient because his wife was back, probably right there listening. That's what he wanted to tell her.

*

At five o'clock Lynne's car pulled up. Cameron opened the door and watched Lynne run across the lawn.

"The director of Steinnman Gallery called," she shouted. "They want to rep me in New York. It's what I've been working for all these."

Lynne grabbed Cameron around the waist, hugging and dancing her up the steps into the living room. "Where's Michael?" she asked.

"He left this morning. Drove to Atlanta. Nell's there. I'm waiting for him to call."

Lynne put both hands on her hips and planted her feet. "If there's one person you can count on, it's him." She lowered her eyes and looked away quickly, too quickly Cameron thought.

"What's wrong?"

Lynne slumped in a chair and closed her eyes.

"What's wrong?" Cameron repeated.

"Damn it," Lynne said. "The happiest day of my life is going to be ruined, but I've got to tell you something. Should of done it a long time ago. I can't stand it any longer, and you're going to hate me." She looked up at Cameron and dropped her face in her hands.

Cameron walked out of the room, then came back and stood over Lynne. "You slept with Mark."

Lynne exploded. "How did you know?"

"Nell tried to tell me there was something going on between you two, but I wouldn't believe her. It happened when you and Mark were in

Atlanta, didn't it?"

"Did Mark tell you?"

"Of course not. I knew there was something wrong because you hardly looked at him after that trip, but he looked at you. I thought you'd gotten into an argument or something, and neither of you wanted to talk about it."

"And you never said anything?"

"I was too stupid to believe you'd sleep with him. You, my best friend."

"When did you find out?"

"For sure? Two minutes ago."

Lynne sunk to the floor. "Jesus. This is awful. Say something. Don't just stand there like it doesn't matter."

"Why should I care? Every man I know betrays me, why not my best friend?" Cameron looked away.

"Don't say that. I didn't betray you. More like I betrayed myself. Mark was no good. He didn't deserve you."

"I know. He's no good, and you're spineless. My husband's bastard just walked out of my life, along with my daughter. That's after Mark tried to rape her, after screwing my best friend, you, and Sanjay's wife is back. Let's see. What else don't I deserve?"

"Sanjay's married?"

"Go away."

"Come on, Cameron. Talk to me."

"He said they were getting a divorce, but

she's back living with him."

"Holy shit," Lynne said. "No wonder you look so awful."

Lynne sat beside Cameron on the sofa. "You're my best friend. Always have been, always will be. I'm an idiot, but I'm going to do better. I never would have had sex with Mark if I hadn't been drunk. I know that's no excuse, but it's the truth." She drew a breath and let it out before she continued. "I'm going to leave Hobetown, but I've got to know that I can come back. That my best friend is still here."

As disgusted as Cameron was with Lynne, the thought of her leaving hurt more than she could have imagined. She leaned back on the cushion, exhausted. Everyone she cared about walked out of her life, and here she sat facing a murder charge.

Lynne went to the kitchen and came back holding the bottle of champagne. "Sanjay's wife is back. That really sucks. I'd like to shoot the bastard." She held up the bottle. "Where'd this come from?"

"Michael. We're supposed to drink it when he comes back, if he comes back."

"Of course he'll come back."

"Like all the other men in my life?"

"He's coming back, Cameron. Get some glasses, and let's drink to that."

Cameron nodded. "We can at least celebrate your good news."

LYNNE

After they finished the champagne, Lynne found the last of the gin. When that was gone, she left Cameron on the steps, pleading with her not to drive home.

"You're going to kill yourself or someone else," Cameron yelled, but Lynne backed the car out of the driveway and sped away. At River Road she slowed down in case Dallas was out cruising. Down the street, the neon sign spelling out Quikie Mart blinked on and off. Lynne pulled to a stop at the door. The night clerk sat behind the counter watching TV, his spidery legs propped on the counter. He watched Lynne walk unsteadily to the cooler and get a six-pack of beer.

"Looks like you've had a few already," he mumbled, his eyes targeting her breasts.

"What's it to you?"

"Hate Dallas to catch you driving drunk."

"I'm not drunk."

"I hear Nell's left town." He unwound his feet and dropped them to the floor.

Lynne drew a ten-dollar bill from her wallet and handed it to him.

Before the clerk took it, he reached down

and adjusted his crotch. "All because of that colored guy."

Lynne didn't respond.

"Cameron ought to know better."

"That had nothing to do with Nell. And the guy is Indian. If you weren't such a dumb redneck you'd know the difference. "

The clerk smirked. "He stopped by here the other day and bought gas."

"How'd you know it was him?"

"How many of them guys you see around here? Had that old man with him. One with the turban." He tossed the change on the counter. "I rode out there last week. Wanted to see that fancy house."

"And?"

"Nothing but a big white box with a wall around it."

"How'd you know it was his house?"

The clerk grabbed his crotch again and grinned, revealing two rows of tobacco-stained teeth, minus a tooth or two. "Heard Dallas talking about it. 'Bout twenty miles up 129. Right past the Baptist church." The clerk leaned across the counter, his eyes fixed on Lynne's cleavage. "Name's on the mailbox." He unwrapped a Tootsie Roll and stuffed it in his mouth. "Even a smart Yankee like you could find it."

Lynne returned to her car and popped open a beer, then sat several minutes sipping it. What would Dr. Rao do if she showed up and told him he was a sleazy lying s.o.b? If Cameron didn't have the gumption to tell him off then she should. The more she thought about it, the more exciting the prospect became. She started the motor and turned around in the direction of highway 129.

When Lynne spotted the mailbox with "S. R. Rao" printed in bold letters, she pulled in the driveway and parked outside the wall. Immediately, floodlights illuminated the area. The front door opened and Sanjay walked outside.

"May I help you?" he called out.

Lynne opened the gate and walked toward him, her steps uncertain.

Sanjay hurried down the walk. "You're Cameron's friend. What's the matter?"

"You're the matter," Lynne fired back. "Why did you lie to her?"

At that moment, a woman walked out the front door. "Is everything okay?"

"It's all right," Sanjay said.

Lynne stared at the woman until she closed the door. Then she approached Sanjay, shaking her finger inches from his nose. "You told Cameron you were getting a divorce."

Sanjay took Lynne's arm and steered her toward a garden bench. "I'd invite you in, but you've had too much to drink, and you need to go home. I'm going to drive you."

"I can drive myself." She tried to pull away, but Sanjay held her.

He called, "Soraya." The door opened again,

and the same woman appeared.

"I'm driving to Hobetown. It'll be late when I get back, but I'll be here in time to see you and Father off. No need to wake him."

CAMERON

Cameron woke to car lights swinging across the living room where she'd fallen asleep on the sofa. Lynne must have decided to come back, but Sanjay opened the door and walked in. Before Cameron could speak he joined her on the sofa and put his arms around her.

"Just be quiet and let me explain. When I was arrested, Soroya, my wife came here to be with my father. He's her great uncle. Arranged marriages are often among extended family members where I come from. She did the right thing to come here. I didn't tell you because you didn't need to be thinking about her, and she was only going be here a few days."

"When is she's leaving?"

"In the morning. Yash is driving her and Father to Miami. She's promised to take him to Disney World on the way."

"But how was I to know that? I haven't seen you since…."

"It's only been three days. I thought you believed me when I said everything would be all right. And …" He took Cameron's face in his hands and looked into her eyes. "It wasn't exactly appropriate for me to be with you until she was gone."

"I was alone and didn't know what was going on."

Sanjay smoothed her hair. "I planned to explain everything tomorrow. I haven't handled this very well, have I?"

Cameron sat up and stared at Sanjay. "Why are you telling me this now? It's the middle of the night."

He grinned and pulled her to him. "It's a long story."

Friday, September 27

MICHAEL

Michael left Haley in bed picking through a tray of pastries. Her hair, shot with streaks of fire, fell around her frothy nightgown. They'd ordered a smörgåsbord of breakfast items from room service and the New York Times which Michael read while Haley surfed the morning's TV programs. He didn't want to leave her, and would have been content to stay in bed all day, but he had to keep his appointment with Hiram Kisker, check on Nell, and find Buford. After that, he intended to come back and take up where they'd left off. "Keep my place warm," he said. Later, he planned to take her across the street to Phipps Plaza and buy her something special, maybe a piece of jewelry, so that every time she looked at it she'd think of him.

*

Hiram greeted Michael with a warm handshake and a slap on the back. "I owe you an apology. I spoke to Curtis this morning. Think I put my foot in my mouth. I must have misunderstood you yesterday."

Michael couldn't imagine what Hiram meant.

"Since I thought you were making a change, I told him I was interested in offering you a job. Of course, I wanted to run it by him before I spoke to you. He said you're marrying his daughter and staying with the firm. I had no idea."

Michael leaned back in his chair and drew in a deep breath. "You don't owe me an apology." He took his time, wanted to get this right. "Mr. Curtis' daughter and I had plans, or at least I did. I hoped we'd get married, and I'd stay in the firm. It hasn't worked out."

Hiram shook his head, dismissing any further conversation with a wave of his hand.

"Nothing would make me happier than to join your firm," Michael said.

"Let's talk about it when you straighten everything out."

Michael floated through the next few minutes before he was jolted back by the news that Hiram had received a call that morning from the director of the High Museum. The Turner painting was a copy, unquestionably one of the finest, but painted fifty years after Turner lived, the work of a notorious forger. Buford was mad as hell and wanted another appraisal.

"There's an interesting caveat to the story,"

Hiram said. "According to the curator, Turner became wildly eccentric as he got older and wouldn't sell his paintings. He had a large fortune when he died and left it all to 'decayed artists'. In spite of that, it ended up at the Royal Academy."

"Wow! Turner's decayed artists and Ms. Ernie's decayed drunks," Michael exclaimed. "They both got short shrift."

"Not entirely. The famous forger's masterpieces are quite valuable. A collector might pay thirty to forty-thousand dollars for one."

"Enough to rehab a shelter." Michael threw his head back and laughed. "In a round about way, Turner's wishes are finally going to be honored."

"I think we underestimated Ms. Gentry. She may have known all along that the painting was a fake. Worth just about what it would take to set up that shelter."

"But Buford thought otherwise."

"Greed carries its own truth." Hiram stood up and offered Michael his hand. "All this over a fake painting."

On his way out Michael stopped in the conference room to call Haley. He wanted her to be the first to know about the possible job offer. There was no answer in the room. He hoped she'd gone to the spa for a massage.

He needed to finish the business with Buford and get back to her. She had to leave tomorrow, and he didn't want the time they had left interrupted with any more of Hobetown's misadventures. Nell could wait. She was probably sleeping anyway, resting up for what would be Callie's last night out after they learned about the painting.

He called Big Mike and explained everything that had happened, including the fact that Haley was at the hotel, and he was eager to get back to her. "I need to take my time, but it's going to work out. I want you to be happy for me."

"I'm happy if you are. Your mother will be, too, but we'll miss you. You've never been that far from home."

"I'll be making enough money to buy a vacation place at the beach or the mountains, and we can all get together somewhere. Mom's going to love Haley."

"If I was you, I'd wait a day or two to tell her, and then only the part about the job offer with that high-falootin' firm. She's got some good news too. Let her tell you hers first."

"She's going to marry that old guy?"

"He ain't so old, but yeah. Said since you was settled it might be time to get married. We're gonna have a party when you get home."

"I'm happy for her. Tell her I said so."

"You better call her yourself."

*

Michael recognized the black Mercedes, like the one he'd seen at Ms. Ernie's house, parked in the lot behind the Peachtree condominium building. He pulled into a space with a view of the door and watched several occupants approach, key in a code and enter. He needed to get in without Buford knowing. A car pulled up beside him and a stylish-looking woman got out. Michael grabbed his briefcase and followed her, far enough behind to give her time to activate the code, then he rushed to hold the door for her. He gave her that "I like the way you look" smile. She returned it, and they stepped into the open elevator. Before she could ask if he was a new resident he patted his briefcase. "I'm here to see Mr. Gentry."

"Oh." She grimaced. "Good luck."

"Is he a neighbor?"

"He lives right above me. Paces like an animal all night."

The door opened on five, and she turned to look at him, a parting glance, before she stepped out. He nodded and punched six. The elevator door closed, and he leaned against the wall, smiling to himself, happy that human nature was so trusting.

He got off on number six. Each floor had four apartments with plaques on the walls conveniently identifying the occupants. He knocked on Buford's door. Inside, he heard footsteps. The door opened, and Buford stood before him in undershirt and sweat pants. He stared at Michael, then closed the door part way and peered through the opening.

"I'm Michael Duncan. I met you at your

mother's house. I'd like to talk to you."

"What do you want?"

"I think you know."

Buford's body jerked. His myopic eyes behind thick glasses darted wildly, and he took a deep breath. "I don't have anything to say to you. Get lost." But Michael already had his foot in the door.

"This won't take long. We can straighten out the whole problem down in Hobetown if you'll give me a minute."

"I don't have a problem."

"You do now." Michael pushed his way through the opening.

Buford stood back and Michael entered a spacious room, the walls covered in huge paintings. Curtains drawn. The air was heavy with the stink of cigarettes and neglect.

"I'm working with Hiram Kisker. We know you persuaded Nell to take the painting."

Buford paced the room, stopping to light a cigarette before putting out another. "Supposing I did. It's my painting."

"Not according to your mother's will."

"That's ridiculous. Any court would overturn that."

"You weren't going to take a chance, so you decided to steal it and not go to court."

Buford flailed his arms in the air. "What difference does it make now? The painting's a fake." Flecks of spittle formed at the corner of his mouth. "I grew up guarding this family secret. We owned a genuine Turner. My great-grandfather bought it in 1861 instead of converting his money to confederate dollars. I have the receipt and the document of authentication. He was swindled, just like I am today."

"Then why don't you come clean? Let the DA know that it was you who took the painting."

"There's the eyewitness." Buford scoffed.

"Forget about the eyewitness. Tell the DA that you were the first one to speak to Billy. He told you that he saw your mother fall through the railing. He was the only one around. That's all it would take. Anything he said to the Chief of Police after that would be thrown out of court." Michael watched Buford's expression, looking for any hint of surprise. "I figure you arrived a few minutes before the police. Too late to get the painting out of the gallery."

"You think you're so clever, don't you?" Buford resumed pacing, swearing under his breath. Michael thought of the woman below.

"Why should I get involved now?" Buford fumed. "It's going to be dismissed."

"Because if you don't, we'll put Nell on the stand, and she'll say that you offered her ten thousand dollars to steal the painting. That would look real good in the Atlanta Journal." Michael looked around the walls. "I'm sure your clients, whose fees buy all this art, would like to know that you'd even steal from your own mother."

Buford's nostrils flared. "Isn't the DA going to wonder why I've waited so long to tell them?"

"No. You didn't know what was going on. Say you asked Nell to get the painting. Neither of you knew your mother was in the house. She obviously fell off the porch. Billy was drunk. He saw both women that day and got confused. Everyone knows Cameron didn't murder your mother."

"And you think the DA will believe that?"

"From what I've seen of Hobetown's judicial system, absolutely."

Michael knew he'd won. He couldn't resist sweetening the moment with another thrust of the stiletto. "And it's going to cost you the ten thousand dollars that you promised Nell."

Buford turned on Michael. "Are you crazy? I'm not paying that bitch a penny. Get the hell out of here."

"Make out the check to her and I'll see she gets it."

Buford raised his fist to Michael.

Michael held his ground. "That's cheap to bury this story. It wouldn't begin to pay my fees. Write the check and it better be good."

*

Michael stopped in the hotel gift shop and picked up a dozen tulips. He rode up the elevator picturing Haley's face when he handed them to her.

The door to their room was ajar and he pushed it open to find a maid at work.

"I'm looking for the lady," he said.

"Haven't seen anyone, sir."

Haley's suitcase was gone. He walked in the bathroom. Everything of hers had been removed. He rushed back to the bedroom. The maid held out a piece of paper. "This was on the dresser."

Michael took the folded note and read: "Your fiancée called."

Before he could ask the maid to leave him alone, she left the room, quietly closing the door behind her.

He leaned back in the chair and closed his eyes. This wasn't the end of the world, he told himself. He could straighten it out. He phoned the front desk and learned that Haley had left an hour earlier. She had a three-hour drive, and he wanted a message to be waiting when she arrived home, so he called her number and when her answer machine picked up he quickly blurted out, "Don't hang up. Just listen to what I say. That was not my fiancée. I don't have one. I do have some unfinished business I will take care of tomorrow when I get home. I've got great news. I'm going to work for Hiram Kisker here in Atlanta. It'll take a little time to get settled, you need time too, then you and Mindy are going to move here, and we're getting married. I'm taking charge, just like you told me to. I'll call you back this evening, and we'll talk about it. I love you, Haley, and I intend to spend the rest of my life with you."

He hung up the phone and fell back in the chair, exhausted. Although the room was cool, perspiration snaked down his neck. His forehead felt hot. Fever. Nausea churned in the pit of his stomach. He needed a short nap, a couple of aspirin, and a shower. Then he must find Nell.

*

He hadn't been asleep more than twenty minutes when the phone rang. He grabbed it, hoping it was Haley, but Nell's voice shrieked from the receiver. "Come get me. Callie's husband is here. They're fighting. Going to kill each other."

Michael rolled over and took a deep breath before he answered. "Go across the street to the diner. I'll be there as soon as I can. Go now!"

Nell was waiting inside the diner door when Michael drove up, and she ran out and jumped in the car. He backed up and drove down the street.

"They're crazy," she wailed. "First she's yelling at me; then she and Joe are accusing me of trying to cheat them out of Callie's money; then they're at each other's throat. Callie went nuts when Buford called and said the painting was a fake and forget about the money."

"When was that?"

"This morning. He said that if I tried to involve him, he'd see to it that I ended up in jail. Keep my mouth shut. Then Joe walked in looking for his car, and they started fighting."

"Calm down. Everything's going to be all right. Mr. Kisker will get the charges dismissed."

"He better." Nell crumpled in the seat. "I just want to go home."

"I can't take you. I've got a plane to catch in the morning."

"Maybe Mom will come get me."

"That's a long drive, Nell. Why don't you surprise her and take a bus?"

"You mean like a Greyhound?"

Michael laughed at the look of shock on Nell's face. He reached in his pocket and handed her the check "Compliments of Buford Gentry."

"Oh my God," Nell yelled. "Oh my God. Ten thousand dollars."

"You can take that to the bank and get a loan to start your cleaning business—without Callie."

Her eyes lit up. "Bet my grandmother would help me. She's really smart. Oh my God. I can't believe it."

Michael turned his attention back to the road in time to see a green pickup flying through the intersection directly at his car.

Nell screamed. Airbags exploded. Glass shattered. Silence.

CAMERON

Since Sanjay left just before sunrise Cameron had walked around the house like a lovesick teenager replaying every moment of the night they'd had together. Fate was handing her a new life, one she never could have imagined. Sanjay finally admitted that Lynne's drunken foray sent him pounding on her door in the middle of the night. Cameron's first reaction was anger, but as the day wore on, the irony of it replaced irritation. Besides, she was happy for Lynne. A place in the Steinmann Gallery's stable assured financial success and probably fame. She'd meet new people; have a real life, maybe even meet a nice guy who'd treat her right. Cameron wouldn't miss her as much now that Sanjay was in her life. Still, what was it going to be like after all these years to lose her best friend?

Cameron answered the phone, expecting to hear Sanjay's warm voice, but when he spoke the sound was hollow, barely audible. "Hiram Kisker called a few minutes ago. There's been an accident. Michael and Nell are in the hospital. They found Kisker's card in Michael's pocket and called him."

"Are they okay?"

"He didn't say. Thinks we should come right away. I'll pick you up in an hour."

While she waited for Sanjay, she called information for Atlanta hospital phone numbers. It took three tries before she found that they'd been admitted to Atlanta Memorial. All she learned was that both patients were in the ER.

She ran out the door when Sanjay pulled up.

"It's really bad, isn't it?" she said, sliding in beside him. "You're not telling me everything."

"Mr. Kisker said not to waste any time. He was very upset. That's all I know."

*

An hour outside of Atlanta they stopped for coffee and Sanjay called the hospital. Nell had been sent to room 3012, but Michael was still in the ER. After that they rode in silence.

It was midnight when Cameron tiptoed into Nell's room and found her sleeping fitfully, her face pocked with tiny cuts from the broken windshield, her eyes black and swollen. The nurse said her injuries were minor, a mild concussion, no broken bones or deep lacerations. She'd probably be released the next day. Cameron wrote a note and put it on the night table. "I'm here in the hospital and will see you shortly. I'm so grateful you're going to be okay. Love you, Mom."

Sanjay waited in the hall, and they rode the elevator down to the Emergency Room. When the door opened, Sanjay's face lit up in recognition. Hiram Kisker was leaning against the desk talking to the nurse.

"How is he?" Cameron asked. "Can we see him?"

"I'm waiting for the doctor to come out," Hiram said. "I haven't spoken to any of them for the last hour."

For the remainder of the night, they sat in the waiting room, eyes fixed on the swinging doors, hoping that the next green scrub suit or white coat would approach them, but all passed, sending looks their way that were impossible to read.

At seven A.M. a doctor entered the waiting area and approached Hiram. He introduced himself, shook hands and in a solemn voice said they'd done all they could to save Michael. The injuries were much too severe. He had been placed on life support.

"Who speaks on his behalf?"

Hiram answered. "His grandfather is on his way from Boston. He should be here later this morning." The doctor asked if they'd like to see Michael, but Hiram declined and said that if there were nothing more he could do, it would be best if he left.

"Someone should be with him," Cameron

said and followed the doctor back through the swinging doors.

Michael's face was nearly unrecognizable. A ventilator pumped air into his chest that could no longer breathe on its own because his neck had been broken by the impact. The moment they removed the ventilator, Michael would be declared dead. His body was warm, and Cameron thought she felt a sensation when she took his hand in hers and placed it on her face.

Sanjay stood behind her, his hands on her shoulders. "I'll stay with you?"

She shook her head. "No need. I'll sit with him 'til his grandfather comes."

"That's going to be quite a while."

"I can't leave him alone."

Cameron must have fallen asleep. She opened her eyes to see an elderly man with a crown of white hair standing at the foot of the examining table, tears streaming down his face. He made no attempt to wipe them away.

"You must be his grandfather," she said. "I am so sorry." She wanted to say more, but she couldn't force the words through her aching throat. She rose and gave him her chair.

"We'll be taking him home," he said. "His mother will want to bury him there." He looked up at Cameron, his expression kind but firm. "It's best if you leave this to me. I appreciate all you've done, but it would be easier if it was just me and him."

Cameron didn't want to leave him, but this was his grandfather's decision. Michael wasn't her son, and she had no right to intrude into the most private moment in this family's life.

*

Cameron waited until noon to walk into Nell's room and face what had to be said. Nell sat on the edge of the bed, swinging her legs. "Where have you been?" she cried. "I've been waiting hours for you. How's Michael?"

Cameron vowed she wouldn't break down when she saw Nell. She pulled up a chair and sat quietly until she could control her voice.

Nell began crying. "He's dead. Oh my God, he's dead. I killed him."

"No, Nell, a drunken fool in a pickup killed him."

"It's my fault. I told him to come get me. Callie and Joe were fighting and…."

"Don't do this, Nell."

"You wish it was me, don't you? You wish I'd been killed instead of Michael."

Cameron wrapped her arms around her daughter. "Don't say that. I'm heartbroken over Michael, of course I am, but you're my daughter. No one could replace you."

"I'm so sorry," Nell cried out. "I wanted to do something good for a change. Just once I wanted people to look at me and say, Nell Patterson is really something."

"You are, Nell. We'll get through this, and things are going to change. We owe Michael that."

Nell stared over Cameron's shoulder, her eyes wide with surprise. Steve stood in the door, a bouquet of gift shop flowers clutched in his hand. "Come in," Cameron stammered. She looked back at Nell who'd pulled the sheet over her head. Cameron grabbed her pocketbook and headed toward the door, patting Steve on the shoulder as she left.

HALEY

Haley didn't think there could be one more drop of water left in her body to cry over that slick-talking, deceiving, good-for-nothing Michael, but every time she remembered how gentle he'd been, how thoughtful and loving he was, she burst into tears. She had no one but herself to blame. After the heartache of Mindy's father she'd sworn off men, agreeing with most of her girlfriends that you can't trust any man under eighty unless he's your father, and that didn't always work out either.

But Michael had been different. She'd have bet the rest of her life on him. And then that bitchy girl called. She didn't bother to say her name, just wanted to know who answered the phone, and why was she in Michael's room. Said she was his fiancée. She had that snarky Yankee accent that right off told you she thought she was better than you. Haley was glad she hadn't given the bitch any satisfaction. All she'd said was that she thought he could be reached at Hiram Kisker's office and hung up. Then she packed her clothes and got out of there. Halfway home she realized how hungry she was and stopped at a roadside diner. She wanted a hamburger and fries. The diner was almost empty, and she sat at the counter. The waitress frowned.

"I know," Haley said. "I look awful."

"You've either lost your dog or your man," the waitress said spreading a toothy grin. "Seeing how pretty you are, I'll bet it's a man."

"How come women are so stupid? Wouldn't you think we'd eventually learn that you can't trust any of them?" Haley sighed.

"You'd think so, honey, but it don't seem to work that way."

When Haley opened the door to the Airstream, the answering machine light flashed on and off. She'd bet anything that the message was from Michael with some lame excuse why his fiancée called and how he was getting ready to break up with her because he didn't love her and why Haley should give him a little time, all that BS men were so good at. In the end, he'd marry that hateful-talking girl, and Mahala Collins Weaver would still be sitting right here in this old trailer. She ought to erase it, not listen to the first word of his lies.

She needed to check on Mindy. If everything was all right there, she'd let her spend the night with her grandmother. She was too tired and depressed to face them tonight. They'd want to know everything. She needed sleep. She hadn't had much of that the last two nights.

She took a hot shower and got into her nightgown before she listened to the message. After the tenth time she played it back, she began to cry, but happy tears this time. She and Mindy would be living in Atlanta with the kindest, sweetest man in the world, her man. Finally, she crawled in bed, as tired and happy as she'd ever been, and fell asleep.

By ten-thirty the next morning he hadn't called. She was about to go crazy when the phone rang. The male voice on the other end sounded weak and old. "Haley," he said. "This is Big Mike, Michael's grandfather."

Made in the USA
Columbia, SC
05 January 2022